MONKEY KING'S REVENGE

By Oliver Eade

Illustrations by Alma Dowle

$d\!p$ Delancey Press
London 2011

Published by Delancey Press Ltd
23 Berkeley Square
London W1J 6HE
www.delanceypress.com

First published 2011

Cover illustration by Alma Dowle
Designed and typeset by Alan Simpson
Printed and bound in the UK by 4edge Ltd, Hockley.

A CIP catalogue record for this title is available from the British Library

ISBN 978-1-907205-16-3

ACKNOWLEDGEMENTS

I am grateful to David Jones for proofreading the text and to all those children at schools and libraries in the Scottish Borders, East Lothian, Perthshire and Houston, Texas, whose kind words about Moon Rabbit encouraged me to right this sequel. Particular thanks are due to Rachel Liu whose idea of 'dragon sparkle' gave me the inspiration I needed to get started.

Dedicated to Yvonne Wei-Lun

Monkey King's Revenge is the sequel to *Moon Rabbit* (November 2009, Delancey Press), a winner of the Writers' and Artists' 2007 Yearbook New Novel Competition and long-listed for 2008 Waterstone's Children's Book Prize.

In *Moon Rabbit*, Scottish Borders schoolboy, Stevie, befriends pretty new Chinese classmate, Maisie, after she gets teased for being different and speaking with a funny accent. Imagining himself to be a Roman legionary, together with his friends Andy and Amy, he decides it's his job to protect the girl. Their *yin yang* friendship enters a new phase when Maisie falls into the River Tweed. Stevie dives in to rescue her but they emerge in mythological China. As White Tiger and Princess Hua-Mei ('Pretty Flower' or Mei), they learn that only the miserable Blue Dragon can tell them how to get back to Peebles but they must first retrieve his magical red pearl and golden staff stolen by Monkey King. They finally succeed, after a dangerous journey across ancient China in which they encounter a grumpy White Crane, a mystical, lucky creature, the Qilin, *gui* or hungry ghosts, Lord Buddha and, of course, Mr Moon Rabbit. The children trick Monkey King into watching Mei dance when, entranced by the girl's beauty, the monkey is caught by White Tiger. They get back the red pearl and golden staff, but the King swears revenge on Mei.

Back in modern day Peebles, Stevie and Maisie move on to High School, having forgotten about the Monkey King until …

Praise for *Moon Rabbit*:

- *Moon Rabbit* will lead children's imaginations to fantastical realms … a magical mix enhanced by gentle and ethereal illustrations … *Mairi Hedderwick, author of Katie Morag books.*

- 'Magical' is the word for *Moon Rabbit* … *Elizabeth McNeill, writer.*

- A roller coaster read … *Inayat Khan, aged 11.*

- A fantastic introduction to Chinese culture and legends … *Gloria Leung, Edinburgh Chinese School.*

- A magical and many-layered, thought-provoking tale, told with a quirky humour and gentle humanity, that will delight children and adults alike. *Barbara Mellor, best-selling writer and translator.*

- As well as being an exciting read, Moon Rabbit has much to offer in considerations of responses to diversity … *Headteacher Update.*

- … magical and captivating … dreamy illustrations … weaves Chinese legends and traditions into an entertaining story of two children from different cultures being brought together … perfect to be read aloud and enjoyed by children of all ages … *Jessica Francis, Sunday Express.*

- Gentle adventure which should appeal to primary aged boys and girls, begins with a situation unfortunately familiar to many children – racial bullying. Oliver handles all themes with dexterity and understanding and has produced a memorable tale … *Parenting Without Tears*

As in *Moon Rabbit*, Chinese words are Romanised using pinyin.

CONTENTS

PRONUNCIATION OF PINYIN

Chinese words are Romanised as 'pinyin':

- *'Qi'* sounds like 'chee...' as in cheese. Universal life-force that flow strongly when the Yin Yang balance is right. *Qilin* is a mythical creature made up from different animal parts (chimera) that appears to an important person at time of need.

- *'Xi'* as in 'she'. *Xiexie*, thank you, sounds like 'sheer sheer'.

- In *'Zai jian'* (Good bye!) the *'ai'* sounds like 'ie' in pie.

- 'Mei', the most important character in the story, is pronounced 'May'. 'Hua' in Hua-Mei, her full Chinese name, is pronounced 'Hwah'.

- *'Zh'* in Hangzhou is pronounced like 'j', and *'ou'* like 'o' in 'Jo'. Thus it sounds like 'Hangjo'.

- The *'ao'* in *'ni hao'* sounds like 'ow' in cow. Think of 'knee how!'

- The *'u'* in *'Kung Kung'*, maternal grandfather, is pronounced the same way as in 'cuckoo'. Same with *Kung fu*, a Chinese martial art.

- In *Feng Shui* ('wind water'), the *'ui'* sounds like 'way'. In Chinese culture, good *Feng Shui*, heaven and earth balance, releases *qi* energy, the life-force.

PROLOGUE

Long ago, before humans existed, four ocean dragon gods bowed in front the Jade Emperor.

"We need more rain," said the Jade Emperor. "We must prepare this world for the coming of the humans, and we must provide them with food. We need more rain to grow it."

"It is our pleasure, your Highness," replied the dragons.

They hesitated and exchanged looks.

"Do we really have to retreat permanently to heaven when the humans come? We like Earth."

"Of course! Who knows what will happen if they see us. They will be terrified. Or they'll annoy us. We shall stay in heaven. Do not disobey!"

They shrank back, all convinced except for Ao Shun, the God of the North Ocean. He was very concerned that when the humans came they would harm his beloved ocean and his beautiful rivers. Ao Shun crept into the River Yangtze and crouched at the bottom. From here he could protect his beloved territory, but he fell asleep.

Years passed, and still Ao Shun slept. After a while, humans began to build villages around the river and the land changed. Gradually, the ocean dragon god drifted out to sea and ended up in a small Scottish river, leaving behind a magic trail of dragon sparkle which travelled through time across the world.

Rachel Liu, aged 12 years,
winner of Delancey Press Moon Rabbit Competition, 2010

CHAPTER 1: MISSING

Stevie Scott awoke with a start. His bed was shaking like his mum's spin dryer and the white ceramic tiger Maisie gave him on turning twelve was doing a little dance on his bedside cabinet. A few seconds later, everything went still. He glanced at his watch. Not yet six, although outside the day was well under way.

With the dawn chorus replaced by a distant hum of vehicles on the Edinburgh road, it seemed as if going back to sleep was missing out on life. Maisie's dad always took the Edinburgh bus shortly after seven, and Stevie and Maisie usually met up after she and her father had finished *Tai Chi* practice by the river. The boy closed his eyes and tried to imagine what they might do together before school that day. He found this easier with closed eyes for he saw her face better.

Seeing her face, he remembered! He kicked off the duvet, scrambled out of bed and ran to the window. Everything appeared so quiet, so normal, but that shaking had been far from normal. It reminded Stevie of Maisie's description of an earthquake she'd experienced when visiting her aunt in southwest China near the Himalayas ... and of the girl's terror of monkeys.

More than a year had passed since Maisie fell in the River Tweed and Stevie dived in to rescue her, emerging in ancient China as White Tiger. If it hadn't been for that first letter, left by

1

the Jade Emperor's messenger underneath a stone at their Chinese-Roman camp, they might have believed their magical journey to retrieve the Blue Dragon's stolen red pearl and golden staff from the spiteful Monkey King was only a shared dream. The letter confirmed it was much more than that.

Stevie knew something mysterious bound him and Maisie together as White Tiger and Princess Hua-Mei. Inseparable as *Yin* and *Yang* (*thanks for that, Mr Moon Rabbit*, thought Stevie ... *cool one!*), they often shared dreams, discussing them down by the river before school. Sometimes these involved further travels in China, and occasionally ancient Rome, for before Maisie came to Scotland Stevie and his friend Andy liked to imagine they were Roman legionaries keeping order in the Scottish Borders. Now they'd become Chinese legionaries and Maisie loved to tell Stevie about China. Stevie, on the other hand, talked about his writing. He'd taken to writing stories about himself and Andy fighting in ancient China and valued Maisie's opinion on everything he wrote.

Since Christmas, Maisie always brought along her yellow notebook with a red flower on the front cover. Stevie had bought it for her since he knew the Chinese imperial colour to be yellow and the flower suited because her Chinese name, Hua-Mei, meant Pretty Flower. It had a small yellow pencil tucked into its spine and Maisie would write down bits of his stories in her notebook or show him things in Chinese calligraphic writing.

Then came the second letter...

That fateful day, a few weeks back, was Maisie's twelfth birthday ... or thirteenth by Chinese counting. Maisie had teased Stevie, saying she was a year older than him although he'd been born two weeks before her.

"How can you be born one year old?" he asked.

"Chinese custom!" she replied, giggling. He loved her giggle.

Stevie had brought along his latest tale about a great battle in ancient China and was about to read it to Maisie when the girl interrupted him. She'd spotted the corner of another letter peeping out from under the same stone. Unfolding the yellowed sheet of paper, she stared at the Chinese calligraphy. He couldn't understand why her hand trembled as she read it but the terror written across her face when she looked up at him told the boy something was horribly wrong.

"What's the matter, Princess?" he asked. When alone together, Stevie always called Maisie either 'Princess' or, more simply, Mei.

"Very bad thing," she replied, on the verge of tears.

"What? Tell me! Is it from the Jade Emperor? Has the Blue Dragon got himself into trouble again?"

The girl shook her head.

"Writing different. See! Say 'you will dance again for me only ... this time forever!'"

Stevie took the letter. Although unable to read Chinese, he could tell the calligraphy was not the same as the last one. It was spiky, untidy, impatient ... and mean.

"Monkey King! I know it," she added.

"Can't *possibly* be the Monkey King." Stevie tried to sound reassuring. "We left him in Buddha's hands. Remember?"

"Buddha not prison!"

The boy felt angry. If Maisie was right, how could Lord Buddha allow the spiteful simian to invade their normal world in Peebles? They'd had such great times since becoming friends. Of course, he and Maisie never saw eye to eye over her religion – the girl had become Buddhist since meeting Lord Buddha on Mount Tai Shan – but they never argued about it. So what, he thought! He was Christian. No big deal! Besides, arguing with Maisie would've been pointless since Stevie only ever wanted her to win.

Both attempted to forget the letter but, whenever alone, Stevie would harp back to it and he could often tell from Maisie's expression she too was worrying. Even the word 'monkey' caused her pretty eyes to widen with fear.

The boy nearly fell over in his haste to get dressed and he never stopped running till just yards from their riverside camp. What he saw stopped him dead in his tracks. Maisie's school skirt and top were there on the log where they usually sat and talked – her shoes neatly placed beside the log – but no Maisie! He dived into the water and swam below the surface, frantically darting this way and that, periodically surfacing for air, searching every square inch of river bed till exhausted.

Sopping wet, he ran with Maisie's clothes to her house. He banged on the door until Mrs Wu appeared. Already distressed her daughter was missing, she was horrified to see the girl's skirt and top in Stevie's hands and totally unable to comprehend the boy's garbled account of her getting kidnapped by the Monkey King. Soon the Wus' house was filled with police officers, neighbours and Stevie's parents. Mrs Wu became hysterical, defying all attempts by Stevie's mum to calm her down, and Stevie was questioned over and over again ... the same question:

Why had he returned from the river with Maisie's clothes and no Maisie?

Everyone knew about their camp. Stevie's father often grumbled about him being too old to play make-believe, childish games; after all, they were almost teenagers, he would remind his son with obvious irritation. Now, *because* they were 'nearly teenagers', people implied he'd done the unthinkable to Maisie. They were accusing him of having harmed her. How could they?

Stevie responded by losing his temper ... *not* a good thing to do to a police officer!

"Yes, I know we're growing up and will soon be teenagers! And of course I know all about girls! D'you have to be so stupid?"

Later, at the police station, the social worker was even worse. She said he *must* tell her about their bust up and 'what he'd done to the girl'.

Done to Maisie? Stevie flipped! He hit red and in his mind's eye he saw the red of Maisie's dance dress as the poor girl was forced to dance forever for the hideous Monkey King.

"IF YOU DON'T GET ANDY, AMY AND ROSIE HERE AT ONCE I'LL CALL ON THE BLUE DRAGON TO WRECK EVERY POLICE STATION IN THE BORDERS!" he shouted. Without a gentle pinch from Maisie to calm him down, what else could he do?

Andy, Amy and Rosie, were co-legionaries. Rosie, now a good friend of Maisie, had recently joined them. A couple of years previously she'd had a boil on the end of her nose. Girls in her class had teased her and that's how she'd come to join up with class bullies, Crazy Davie and Muckle Mikey. But Maisie made sure Amy and the boys never again called her 'Red-Nosed Rosie' for there was nothing wrong with her nose and the girl would no longer be seen dead with those two wasters.

Like the other three legionaries, she'd seen both letters and would vouch for Stevie. All four children gave the same story to the social worker and the police, accusing everyone involved of doing nothing to save Maisie from the Monkey King. They were finally freed and allowed to get on with the important job of working out how to get to ancient China. Meanwhile, a nationwide appeal for the Chinese girl was launched. Images of her appeared everywhere, on notice-boards, on TV and in newspapers. The assumption that Maisie had been abducted, hurt, even murdered, fanned Stevie's anger although he doubted murder had been on the monkey's mind.

Half a day had already been wasted at the police station and Stevie felt an escalating urgency to get back to mythological China. But *how*? The children were horrified to see police frogmen still dragging the river when they went there to look for clues. Stevie, who knew they'd not find a body, was about to give up searching when Rosie ran to the water's edge and scooped something into her hands.

"What's this?" she asked, showing him her find.

The others came to take a look. In Rosie's hand were three sparkling points of coloured lights. The weather was cloudy, so whatever glittered in the girl's palm was not reflecting sunlight.

"What on earth *is* it?" she repeated.

No one knew. Each sparkle seemed almost alive as the girl's hands shone with dancing rainbow patterns.

"Must've got disturbed by the frogmen!" suggested Stevie. "Doubt it's anything to do with Maisie disappearing ... but hang on to it, Rosie. Just in case. Keep it in your hankie."

"I don't have ..."

Stevie handed her his handkerchief.

"We're wasting time," said Andy. "*Every*one knows King Arthur and his Knights are hidden inside the Middle Eildon Hill. They could do magic and stuff. With Merlin. Bet he's the only guy able to get us to ancient China. I'll find a spade in dad's shed and ..."

"Idiot!" accused Amy.

They all knew about Andy's recent obsession with King Arthur and medieval heraldry.

"Hey, just pull together, dudes, and keep focussed, can't you?" begged Stevie.

"Not my fault if Andy comes up with such crass ideas!"

"Okay ... *this* is what we'll do! I'll go with Rosie to the Chinese restaurant. They may be able to help. We'll show 'em Rosie's sparkly dust."

"Why does it have to be you and *Rosie*?" pouted Amy. "Anyway, the restaurant might be closed!"

"Don't care. I'll bang on the window. See whether the Chinese woman there can tell us if Rosie's funny stuff has anything to do with ancient China. Amy, you go dig the Eildon Hills with Andy. Who knows? He might be right. No other leads!"

Stevie, loyal to his friend, took every opportunity to help

Andy woo Amy, the 'love of his life', although the wooing never seemed to work.

"Can't Rosie go with Andy?" Amy suggested. The other girl's eager expression showed that for a change she was in full agreement with Amy. "She's always trying to make excuses for him!"

"No mutiny! *Please*! Just think about ..." Stevie turned his face away. He didn't want them to see his eyes moisten. "Think about Maisie! Right?"

All had sensed the tremor early that morning. Their parents and the police accused them of talking rubbish when they suggested this had something to do with Maisie's disappearance.

"Peebles is most definitely not on a fault line, so it must've come from China," Stevie insisted. "A sort of earthquake! And *we* felt it 'cos something opened up a door between us and ancient China when the Monkey King came to steal Maisie. Like the Jade Emperor was letting us know."

"Could've been King Arthur and his knights stirring in the Eildon Hills," offered Andy. "In their sleep, perhaps."

Amy groaned.

"Can't you keep him under control?" she asked.

Rosie frowned.

"Keep *yourself* under control! Stop being so mean to Andy. Maybe he's got a point about King Arthur. No one knows what lies buried under the Eildon Hills!"

Andy looked downcast. If only *Amy* would stand up for him like that ... as if he was *her* hero, not Rosie's. Whenever Stevie spoke she went all gooey-eyed, but *he* only had to open his mouth and she'd accuse him of spouting rubbish.

"Seriously! Something weird must've happened when they took Maisie," added Stevie. "A time-space thing, perhaps?"

So Stevie and Rosie set off for the Chinese restaurant in the hope that someone there might know the origin of the sparkly rainbow dust, whilst Andy and a reluctant Amy were driven to Melrose and the Eildon Hills by Andy's ever-tolerant elder brother, Ross, armed with a garden shovel. All agreed Maisie had been abducted by the vengeful Monkey King. None expected ever to see her again, and worst hit was Stevie for whom the Chinese girl had become more of a soul-mate than a friend.

CHAPTER 2: DRAGON NOODLE

"You shouldn't let Amy go on like that about Andy," Rosie admonished Stevie. "She's so mean! Only puts him down 'cos she's keen on you."

"What's that?" Stevie's mind was somewhere else.

"Anyway, perhaps he's right about King Arthur."

"Andy? Yeah, Andy's okay! Just a little ... well, different, I s'pose. Good legionary, though."

"D'you think the Monkey King will harm Maisie? Do those horrid things they talked about in the police station?"

"I don't want to *think* about it! Curses! Restaurant's closed. *Hell!*"

"There's someone in there. Look! Sitting by the window."

"That funny old guy? Never seen him before. *She's* there, though. The Chinese lady who does our takeaway!"

Stevie knocked on the window to catch her attention. It worked. She opened the door, her face aglow with that usual friendly smile.

"Hi children! Hungry already? Today special menu. Dragon noodle! You want try?"

"Um ... not exactly hungry. See, we wondered ... like wanted to know ..." began Stevie.

"Come in! See menu. But why no want dragon noodle?"

Stevie and Rosie followed her into the restaurant.

"What's this, please?" asked Rosie deciding there was no

point in beating about the bush. Removing her hankie, she opened out it to show the woman the three glowing points.

"Yes! Like I say ... dragon noodle! Special!"

"No, you don't understand. We wondered what this sparkly stuff is."

"Like does it have anything at all to do with ancient China?" added Stevie.

"Me no understand? *You* no understand! Dragon noodle! Ask *him*!"

"Who?"

With a slight turn of her head, the smiling woman indicated the still figure seated like a statue in a corner by the window. Rosie and Stevie gawped at an elderly Chinese gentleman with bright eyes, white hair, a droopy moustache and goaty beard. He reminded Stevie of the old guy in one of the Chinese scroll paintings on the wall in the Wus' living room. When Maisie had informed him the man was a sage, he'd told her sage was what you put in turkey stuffing, together with onions, at Christmas. The girl had laughed, but insisted a sage was a wise man. Later, the dictionary confirmed both to be right.

"Show *him*! He like see!" the woman said.

Rosie cautiously approached the man who, though staring straight at her, also appeared to be looking *through* her at something way in the distance, and his face showed no expression whatsoever ... like in that painting.

"Um ..." she began timidly, offering him a glimpse of the points of light in the hanky.

The old fellow nodded wisely. Stevie, reminded of both sages and Maisie, felt his sadness become unbearable. Would he ever see the girl again? As for her and the Monkey King being together, he'd once lost his temper when she'd told him how Crazy Davie had asked her out to the movies in Galashiels. Although she'd turned the other boy down, and had never once given Stevie cause for concern, he realised for the first time that nothing was certain. *This* is what had made him angry rather than Davie asking her out. He wanted the thing between him and Maisie always to be certain.

The thought of never seeing her again, and her being alone with the Monkey King, made him furious with the old man for having such a vacant look on his face. Sages were supposed to be wise, not daft!

"Look, whoever you are, sir, Rosie's asking you if you know what this stuff is. It might help us find Maisie Wu. The missing girl! Didn't you hear it on the news? She *is* Chinese, you know!"

"Chinese *princess*!" corrected the man.

Stevie pricked up his ears. Only he and his friends called her 'Princess'.

"Like lady tell you. Dragon noodle!"

"What are you on about?"

"Long noodle made from dragon sparkle. Travel anywhere, time or space. Come from ancient dragon, long ago. Dragon sparkle spill from dragon like trail. Go many places through time. Men once knew this. Men from city called Rome. These men came here. To Scotland. To collect dragon sparkle. Save for future. Make noodle."

Stevie stared with renewed wonder at the sparkle for it began to make sense. What if somewhere hidden on the river bed was a collection of the same stuff, so concentrated it formed

one end of a mysterious 'noodle' of magical light that would link them to the past and to China?

"Yeah … of course! Dragon noodle! Thanks!" he exclaimed. "Helps us a lot. You've no idea!"

"Uh?" queried Rosie, puzzled.

"Never mind! Hurry back to the river. Start looking for our end of the noodle before the others return from Melrose."

"Dragon noodle?"

"You'll see!"

The girl shrugged her shoulders and accompanied Stevie back to the river … wishing he could magically turn into Andy! Why couldn't *Amy* have gone with Stevie if she was that nuts about him?

* * * * *

If only Andy was Stevie, thought Amy as she sat alone in the back of Ross's car wondering how she could be crazy enough to agree to join up with a freak who planned to dig King Arthur and his knights out of the Eildon Hills with a garden spade. She reckoned someone ought to get Ross to sort out his little brother for once and for all. Perhaps he needed the attention of one of those psychiatrist doctors who make holes into people's minds with funny questions.

"I'll sit and read my book here for an hour and half," announced Ross after pulling into the lay-by beside Bowden Loch at the foot of the Eildon Hills. "If you and your girlfriend aren't back by then, together with King Archie and the Arabian knights, I'll call out the Mountain Rescue. Bit of luck they'll ban you from ever setting foot outside the house again!"

"I am *not* his girlfriend!" objected Amy.

Ross paid her no attention. He waved his mobile phone at them.

"Countdown starts now!"

"Hmmmph!" the girl grunted, clambering out of the car. Andy removed the spade from the boot and they made their way to the top of the highest, middle, Eildon whilst Amy denied every alternative to 'girlfriend' that Andy could come up with. 'Pal', 'acquaintance', 'colleague' – even just 'friend' – were all rejected. At the summit she informed him she'd make her way back to Ross in twenty minutes and until then would sit alone on a rock since she had no intention of doing anything so unladylike as digging.

"Okay!" exclaimed Andy. He was so smitten with her he'd agree to anything the girl suggested. "So … um … how about 'special'?"

"Special what?"

"Our relationship. Special! Sounds cool! Like you can get special fried rice at the Chinese restaurant. So … Amy, Andy's *special* friend!"

"Shut up! It sounds stupid!"

She sat and sulked on her rock as Andy dug on, muttering loudly enough for the girl to hear:

"Or mate? Could be my girl mate. No! Girl chum. Yeah! I like it. Andy's special girl chum, Amy!"

"Yuk!"

Andy stabbed and scraped at the tough, stony ground with his spade, as with Amy making no impression whatsoever.

"Why on earth they chose this place to bury themselves, I've no idea!" he complained when he paused for a breather, resting folded arms on the spade handle. "Hey ... what *are* you doing, Amy?"

She'd got up from the rock and was kicking with determination at something in the dirt.

"Trying to work out what I've done wrong to deserve being lumbered with you for the morning. OW!" She'd stubbed her toe and hopped about on the other foot. "Look, come and do something useful for change. Help me with this!"

Andy came immediately, like an obedient puppy.

"What?" he asked.

"There! The thing I was kicking and stubbed my toe on."

"That old stone?"

"It's been carved. Not natural. You can tell. There's letters on it."

Andy got down on the ground and scraped away with his hands. The girl was right. The stone, half-buried buried in the hard earth, had a right-angled edge as if fashioned with a hammer and chisel. A crude D and an R had been chipped onto its rough surface.

"Amy, get my spade! Hurry!"

For a few moments she stood gaping, rubbing her injured toe against the back of her other leg.

"Quick!" he urged, scowling.

To his surprise, the girl hopped off to collect the spade and limped back with it. After Andy had dug around the stone, they used their combined strength to lift the thing from the ground with the flat of the spade. Andy sensed a tingle of delight when their arms briefly touched. Contact with the love of his life at last ... *and* he'd be proved right! He would finally become her hero, for this object surely had something to do with King Arthur.

By the time the ground had yielded up the flat, rectangular stone, they only had half an hour left to get back to Ross and the car. Carrying it between them, they struggled down to the loch.

"Oh my God, what on earth have you got here?" Ross asked his brother, relieving them of their shared burden as if it weighed no more than a Nintendo DS. "Funny writing on it, ay?"

"Not funny! That's an ancient language as used by King Arthur and his knights."

Ross put the stone on the back seat.

"Like hell! Well, your girlfriend can look after King Archie's tombstone, right?"

"Girl *chum*!" corrected Andy. Amy groaned. "And it's King *Arthur*! I thought you were s'posed to be going to university next term!"

Ross dropped them off near the river at Peebles and they carried the stone tablet together to the camp. They were surprised to see Rosie and Stevie standing knee deep in water trawling the river bed with sticks. It hadn't rained much for weeks and the level was low.

"Hey, Stevie, you're wasting time! They've already dragged the river. I've found King Arthur's tablet on the Eildons. He or Merlin will get us to Maisie."

"*I* found it!" objected Amy. "And it's nothing to do with King Arthur. Just a bit of an old tombstone."

"Show us," said Stevie, wading back to the bank.

He helped the others lay the tablet carefully on the ground and rubbed off the dirt with his sleeve.

"Latin!" he proclaimed.

"There! An ancient language. Bet you King Arthur spoke Latin."

Andy's grin stretched from ear to ear.

"Bet he didn't," contradicted Amy.

"*DRACONIS LUMEN* ... er ... light of dragon ... dragon sparkle!" began Stevie, translating the carved out capitals. "Um ...'*ARCA IN FLUMINE* ... box in the river ... '*EST*' ... is ... *TRES PASSUS* ... er ... three paces ... um ... double steps and they're about five feet. So, fifteen feet. That'll be from the bank. *RUPES* ... rock ... under ... um ... dunno ... hidden perhaps?"

The boy rubbed some more.

"There's Chinese characters too. I ken what they mean. Maisie and I were planning a pretend banquet for ... well never mind ... a sort of celebration involving just *us* ... and she wrote things in Chinese next to the English. Used these characters. Mean noodle. *Dragon* noodle."

He turned over the stone.

"Cool, guys! A map! There's the Roman camp at Trimontium. See! And the river ... and the Roman bridge near Trimontium. Been there ... or where it used to be! More camps here ... and there ...see! The noodle sign again. Could be Peebles. You're brilliant, Andy!"

"Keep telling *her* but she won't believe me," responded Andy, jerking a thumb in Amy's direction.

"*I* found it anyway!" Amy flashed her eyes hopefully at Stevie.

"I'll take a chance," continued Stevie. "Water's low. Search the river bed fifteen Roman-sized feet from shore near where

Rosie found the Dragon sparkle and we should find the box. And *our* end of the dragon noodle."

"Noodle?"

"Aye! The old sage Rosie and I met sort of explained it. A noodle of concentrated dragon sparkle. Left behind by one of the first dragons. Travels through time and space. The Romans who came here knew about it. All makes sense."

"Like doughnuts and hairdryers?" Andy suggested, grinning at Amy, but the boy's humour was lost on her.

"Don't make fun of Stevie! Just because it's got nothing to do with King Arthur ..."

"*Wasn't* making fun. Don't you get it? You could cook a doughnut by looping it over the end of a heated hairdryer. Wouldn't normally think of a connection ... so ..."

Amy stared coldly at him.

"Noodles ... dragon sparkle ... Maisie? Oh, never mind!"

"Think I'd better go alone," Stevie sighed with irritation.

"No you won't!" objected Andy, casting an 'I'm-braver-than-you-think' look in Amy's direction. "Legion business! Remember? One for all and all for one? The Three Legionaries?"

"Musketeers!" corrected Amy.

"Me included!" announced Rosie. "*That's* three!" She narrowed her eyes at Amy.

"What if you're all wrong?" questioned the other girl. "I mean, I do wanna help Maisie. She's my best friend. But jumping into the river? Stevie ... they said you and she were nearly dead when Ross fished you out last year."

"That's the point! Our bodies got fished out but Maisie and

I were somewhere else. Together in ancient China at the other end of the dragon noodle. Don't you see?"

"Oodles of noodles in China!" observed Andy. He was the only one who laughed.

"Not sure I'll come if *he's* gonna be with us!" snorted Amy.

Rosie stamped her foot.

"Don't be so *horrid* to Andy!"

"Oh, for heaven's sake, guys, pull together! This is life or death for Maisie. One false move by anyone and she's stuck there forever! Monkey King's prisoner! Amy, trust me. Our bodies stay protected by dragon sparkle, and the 'us' parts are at the other end in ancient China. Like there's already a Chinese us there, but we've gotta travel the dragon noodle to bring it to life. In a parallel world, see!"

"Will I jabber away in Mandarin, then?" asked Andy, lost by his friend's complicated explanation.

"God, that'd be even worse than him jabbering in English!" said Amy. "Anyway, what happens to our clothes? You found Maisie's here. Mum'll kill me if I get my jeans wet ... and I'm not taking anything off in front of *him*!"

She glared at Andy before he could say anything.

"Dunno about clothes," replied Stevie. "Keep 'em on. Maybe they forced Maisie to change back into her red Chinese dance dress before pulling her into the dragon noodle."

Stevie imagined Maisie putting up a fight as she got dragged struggling into the river by a band of monkey warriors. She wasn't one to give in easily.

"I'm going! Come if you want. When I find the dragon sparkle I'll give the thumbs up and dive into the noodle. If I've not resurfaced by three minutes you know I'm okay. Dead bodies are supposed to float. Anyone who wants to join me, follow. I'll wait a short while at the other end. In China!"

He glanced up on hearing sobs. It was Amy.

"It's okay. I'll find her and bring her back."

"It's not that. I wanna come but I can't swim."

"Can't *swim?*" Andy couldn't hide his disbelief. A year back, Maisie was also unable to swim, but Stevie had given her lessons and she now swam like a fish.

"No need to be so superior. Not my fault! My parents never had me taught."

"I'll teach you," offered Andy.

"Rather be taught by a frog," scoffed the girl.

"Cool it, dudes!" warned Stevie. "Amy comes with me if she wants to, otherwise she can remain here at base camp ... and prepare for our return."

"I really do want to be with you."

"But *I* wanna look after her!" exclaimed Andy.

"Everyone takes orders from me!" insisted Stevie. "I'll go first, with Amy. We'll travel through the noodle when I've found the dragon's box. Rosie and Andy can follow. Amy ... practice taking a few deep breaths like this ... then hold your breath."

Reassured the girl could at least do that, Stevie put his arm about her waist (her face lit up!) and they waded into the river. Andy glowered at him. After all, he already had a girlfriend.

Stevie soon spotted what he sought ... a large slab. The frogmen had missed it, doubtless looking for the wrong thing –

a body tied to a weight, perhaps? He shuddered to think Maisie could ever end up like that, although somehow her being imprisoned forever in the Monkey King's palace seemed almost worse.

He kicked at the rock, also engraved with the Chinese characters for 'noodle' and 'dragon'. A fleck of dragon sparkle hovered in the water defying the swift current's attempt to shift it seawards ... the only evidence that it belonged to a different dimension. Unable to dislodge the slab with his foot he dived in and wrestled with it, twisting and turning, but the object refused to budge. He returned to the surface, gasping, fearing his lungs would burst ... seeing not dragon sparkle but stars!

"What's wrong?" called Andy.

"Can't shift the flipping thing," replied Stevie on recovering his breath. "It's the Roman box of dragon sparkle okay but it's like a ton weight. Must've been muckle strong, those Romans, ay?"

"Na! Just clever. Use a lever!"

"A what?"

"Lever. Hang on! We'll break a branch off for you."

"Cool!" exclaimed Rosie, only too eager to assist Andy.

She and Andy disappeared up the path. A loud snapping sound was followed by girlish giggles, and they reappeared dragging a branch. Soon all four kids were up to their thighs in the river and leaning on the branch that Andy had wedged under the ancient stone. It began to shift and they eased it up and over. A sudden burst of dazzling white light shot from the space underneath illuminating their faces whilst a slick of

shimmering dragon sparkle fringed with strange rainbow patterns spread out into the surrounding water.

Andy triumphantly punched the air.

"LONG LIVE KING ARTHUR!" he yelled.

"Oh wow!" Rosie exclaimed, her red hair glowing as if on fire. "I'm coming with you, Andy. Remember?"

"Me and Amy first," advised Stevie, gazing into the depthless white of the large dragon noodle. He grabbed Amy's hand. "Big breaths, girl!"

She breathed in and out till her head went swimmy.

"NOW!" he shouted.

"Go for it, dudes!" urged Andy as Stevie and Amy disappeared into the noodle. "We're right behind you!"

Stevie held firmly onto Amy as they were sucked along, twisting and turning, chasing the brightness ahead. He had no idea which way was up and which down, like when he'd dived in to rescue Maisie the previous year. Swimming swiftly towards the brightness, he wished he was pulling Maisie back to Scotland rather than Amy towards China. Finally they broke water, taking in great gulps of air

CHAPTER 3: THE SNAKE, THE TEMPLE AND THE MONK

Thank goodness!

Stevie breathed a sigh of relief. In front of him stretched a huge lake – West Lake – beside Maisie's home city of Hangzhou as it was a thousand years ago. He helped Amy up onto the bank.

"It's okay," he chuckled. "You can un-pinch your nose. We're here! In China!"

Scanning the lake dotted with Chinese boats, he saw an island ... the same island he and Maisie had looked at ... bearing Chinese people and strangely-shaped buildings. In the distance, across the lake, was a fringe of green mountains. Amy's mouth opened in wonder as she stared at the long blue Chinese dress she now wore.

"You're the Chinese Amy and I'm White Tiger again!" the boy announced, proudly showing off his white shirt with Chinese buttons.

White Tiger heard a splash as they clambered up the steep bank. He turned and saw Andy's head appear above the water.

"HEY ... WHITE TIGER! COOL!" Andy called out.

Moments later, Rosie's head popped up beside him. White Tiger scrambled back down the slope to help his friends out of the water. To Rosie's amazement she was wearing a long pink dress, and Andy, a brown top and trousers.

"Heck!" cursed the boy. "Rubbish clothes! Why couldn't they have me looking like a proper knight?"

White Tiger wasn't listening. As he gazed across the lake at the mountains, China suddenly seemed vast and hostile as well as beautiful. Getting there was only the beginning, for somewhere in that vastness was poor Maisie, now a prisoner of the Monkey King. He didn't even know in which direction they should set out to find her.

The boy rejoined Amy at the top of the bank. She was staring at a town of wooden houses, dusty, narrow streets and happy Chinese children, running around and laughing. Could *he* ever feel happy again should he and his friends fail to find Maisie?

An old fellow sat on his haunches, his back to a wall. Like White Tiger he was dressed in white and was using chopsticks to slurp up noodles from a bowl.

"I'll ask Mr White," White Tiger told the others. "He's the daytime guardian god of Hangzhou. Might know something about Maisie 'cos she comes from Hangzhou. May've seen her being dragged from the noodle. Here she's like a *real* princess. Princess Hua-Mei. That means Pretty Flower, ken?"

"We *know*! You keep telling us! And I'm just a lady-in-waiting!" complained Amy. White Tiger got the uneasy feeling she only wanted to be there because of him and not to rescue Mei. He approached the shabby god who the previous year had named him White Tiger.

"*Ni hao!*"

Mr White looked up, a noodle dangling from his lower lip. He sucked this into his mouth, belched and wiped a grubby sleeve across his face.

"A god?" questioned Andy. "I told you we'd have done better digging up King Arthur!"

"Shhhh! "White Tiger threw his friend an angry glance.

"So, White Tiger! You've come at last!" began Mr White, speaking in English. "What took you so long? Mustering that little army of yours, ay? Know how many fierce fighters the Monkey King has at his disposal?"

"Aye ... well this is only a disguise," Andy tried to explain. "Should see me in my knight's kit! They'd run screaming. I'm telling you, a charging knight is ..."

"Mr White ... did you see Princess Hua-Mei?" interrupted White Tiger.

"See? Not exactly the right word. *Feel*, more like. Monkey King was there himself, you see, and as you know he can clear a thousand *li* in one jump. A few leaps, and he'll have had the princess at his palace. In the dungeon. To keep her safely locked up till he gets the Jade Snake. Terrible place, the dungeon of the Monkey King. Crawling with spiders, cockroaches and rats!"

White Tiger feared for his Chinese girlfriend. He knew how she hated creepy-crawlies.

"What's the Jade Snake?"

"Lies hidden in a temple on the holy mountain of Emei Shan. In the west. Bears a magical curse from which there's no escape. To wear the Jade Snake is a punishment more terrible than being turned into a *gui* (hungry ghost). As soon as the Monkey King places it around Pretty Flower's neck, she'll want to love and obey him whatever he does. The girl will lose all reason. He'll force her to dance till she drops from exhaustion.

Poor princess! She's such a sweet child. We're all in mourning in Hangzhou, you know!"

The word 'mourning' upset White Tiger. You only mourn if something's happened. Not even Mr White knew whether the Monkey King had found the Jade Snake.

"They say he's sent eight *wuya* birds (ravens) to seek it out. Eight for luck."

"Who? *Who* said that?"

"The Jade Emperor's messenger."

"Can't the Jade Emperor stop them?"

Calls himself an emperor? Huh!

White Tiger felt frustrated there was someone in power doing nothing to save Mei.

"Doesn't work like that, White Tiger. Surely you've learned this by now! *You're* her only hope. You and ..." Mr White peered at the other three standing behind White Tiger, "him ... and her ... and *her!*" he added disdainfully, waving his chopsticks at them.

"Tell me about the palace. How can we get there?"

"In the centre of the middle kingdom of *Jongguo*. China to you. More than three thousand *li* (Chinese mile) to the west. On top of a mountain of vertical rock hundreds of feet up towards heaven. Not even a lizard could scale the cliff to the palace. Only trained monkeys. The palace itself has eight levels ... for luck."

Luck? Why does he keep reminding me, like I've run out of it? thought White Tiger.

"Good *Feng Shui*," explained the scruffy god.

Mei had told White Tiger about *Feng Shui* and how the Chinese use this to design homes and buildings that made people feel good and brought them fortune because of alignment with the elements.

"The dungeon is at the bottom level. In the winter it's freezing. No way could Pretty Flower survive. But he'll not want her to die because he really loves her dancing, so he'll have trained the *wuya* birds well. Their eyesight's razor sharp and they'll sweep through that temple like locusts, attacking any monk who dares try to stop them."

"And when he's got the Jade Snake?"

"With her own suite of rooms, she'll be free to wander freely in the palace because then she'll only have eyes for the Monkey King ... longing for the day when she'll change from Princess Hua-Mei into the Monkey Queen."

"Would she ... well ... also *look* like one of them?" White Tiger asked anxiously.

Mr White shrugged his shoulders.

"Dunno! Only that she wouldn't recognise you ... or even her own parents ... and she'd *never* leave him. It'd break her heart."

White Tiger and Mei were so close he couldn't imagine her not knowing him.

"In short, once the Jade Snake's around Pretty Flower's neck you lot might as well slip back to Bonnie Scotland through the dragon noodle ... if there's enough dragon sparkle left. Your friend was so careless he dragged half the stuff out into the lake with him. Look!"

He scornfully indicated a large patch of rainbow glitter shimmering on the water.

"Don't blame me!" objected Andy. "Was showing Rosie how

to do somersaults under water! Awesome, ay, Rosie?"

"Now see what you've gone and done, you nutter!" snapped Amy.

"Stop it! I hate you!"

Rosie, ever ready to defend Andy, stuck her tongue out at Amy.

"Hmmm!" grunted Mr White, returning to his noodles. "Couldn't you have found a better army than this lot?"

"Please sir, I don't mean to be rude ..." began White Tiger.

"Then don't be!"

"If Mei ... Pretty Flower ... really *is* a princess here, can't you help us a little more? Like tell me how to get to the monkey's palace?"

"No! But *she* can!"

"Who?"

"The one who's been so patiently waiting with her sisters ever since you lot came out of the noodle. Over there!"

With a sweep of his hand Mr White took in the whole of the lake.

"Uh?"

"Hope you're not needing glasses! Hard to come by here!"

"What are those big white birds?" asked Rosie, staring at the island on the lake.

Three white cranes stood motionless on a rock beyond a promontory at the end of the island. Even from a distance White Tiger saw their heads were black and red, their wings tipped black, unlike White Crane on whose back he and Maisie had flown the previous year.

"Not 'what', but 'who'!" corrected Mr White. "White Tiger knows all about them yet doesn't bother to ask for their assistance."

Without Mei to give him a gentle pinch to remind him to keep his cool, White Tiger felt his temper slipping dangerously close to the brink. Somehow he managed to refrain from uttering the angry words hovering on his lips.

"Look, Mr White, I'll fill a supermarket trolley with noodles and bring it here free of charge if you could be a wee bit more cooperative!"

"You've got me wrong! Don't need a thing. I'm a god, after all. But *her*?"

"Her?"

"Yeah! The Crane Maiden! One of the three crane sisters who turn into beautiful women on a magical lake! Remember? You could at least offer *her* a reward by promising to reunite her with her son. White Crane told you the story when you and the princess were on your way to the Blue Dragon's cave and they flew past. Keeps me informed, you see."

White Tiger remembered. At first he'd mistaken them for airplanes. Oh, how Mei had enjoyed that flight. When he closed his eyes he could still see that bright smile lighting up her happy face.

"Yeah! Made her laugh when I said they were airplanes," he chuckled. "So they're the ... "

"The princess loves people who make her laugh," interrupted Mr White. "But those birds aren't gonna stand there forever!"

"How do we get to the island?"

"Swim if you like, but with the amount of dragon sparkle your friend scattered about you might end up back in Peebles. Or lose your toes to the hungry pike in the lake. Get Fisherman Yi to take you. He's also being extremely patient."

A short way along the bank stood a fisherman, arms folded, with a smile that looked as if it had been painted permanently onto his face. Strangely, White Tiger hadn't noticed him before.

"Thanks, Mr White. Sorry I'm a bit uptight. Just that ..."

"Yes, yes! You miss the princess, I know. *Yang* without *Yin*, right? Not much *Qi* force left in you? Better get to her quick! Before she ... er ... never mind! Hurry!"

Soon the children were being rowed across the lake towards the three cranes. The birds stood so still White Tiger feared Mr White had been pulling his leg and that they were only statues. Then one stretched her wings, took off and circled a few times before settling on the bow of the boat. Fisherman Yi nodded and smiled at White Tiger. Crane Maiden spoke:

"I'll take *you*, White Tiger, and the one with love in her heart. The other two can go with my sisters. We fly faster than the *wuya* birds ... *much* faster ... but they had a head start. Like three thousand *li*!"

"Hey, *that* bird just spoke!" Rosie gaped, astounded, at Crane Maiden.

"So would you if you'd once been a beautiful woman turned into a crane!"

"Uh?"

"No time to tell you now. Get onto my back with White Tiger! Quick!"

White Tiger climbed onto the Crane Maiden's back and pulled Rosie up behind him as the bird's two sisters landed in the stern. Andy tried to help Amy onto one but she pushed him away.

"Why do I always have to get lumbered with you?" she sneered.

"Simple! 'Cos I'm your knight in shining armour?"

"Shut up! H ... E ... E ... ELP!"

Andy caught the girl as she slipped backwards off the bobbing bird. She maintained a dignified silence whilst he assisted her a second time, advising her to hold on tightly to the creature's neck. He mounted the third crane, informing Amy she'd swoon like she'd never swooned before if she could only see him on a knight's charger rather than a big bird.

"*Zai Jian* (Good bye), White Tiger! Only return when you have the princess!" called Fisherman Yi. The three birds spread their wings and ascended into the air. "May the *Qi* force guide you to her! Remember ... *Yin* and *Yang*!"

White Tiger wished he'd been able to tell Rosie the story of the three cranes fabled to fly to a magical lake where, on shedding their feathers, they'd transform into beautiful women. Once the very crane on which they were perched fell in love with a man she met bathing in the lake. They married and had a child called Zhang, whom she adored, but her husband's jealous mother forced her to turn back into a crane and she lost him forever.

They flew too fast for conversation. Faster even than the mystical *Qilin* who'd helped White Tiger and Mei the previous summer. Almost as fast as when White Crane took them to the moon. Periodically the boy turned to check on Rosie and make sure the other cranes, carrying Andy and Amy, were still behind them. Andy pretended to brandish an imaginary lance at unseen foes whilst Amy clung to the neck of her bird as if the slightest movement might send her plummeting to her death.

Soon they were flying over a wild, forested landscape bristling with tall, tooth-like mountains. The Crane Maiden turned her head.

"The Monkey King's palace is coming up on your right," she said.

White Tiger peered down. Perched on a stony pinnacle stood a vast, fortress-like building with curvy Chinese roofs, turrets and arrow-slit windows … magnificent and indestructible, but he felt only sadness knowing Mei was a prisoner there and he could nothing about it. The turrets were crawling with monkey warriors bearing spears and bows.

"Can't you swoop down? Scatter them or something … so I can rescue Mei?" he asked Crane Maiden.

"We're an easy target, White Tiger. Any closer and you'll be shot through the heart. Couldn't do much dead, ay?" White Tiger agreed. "We've got to intercept the *wuya* birds," she added. "Once the Jade Snake's round her neck it'll be too late. She'll never want to come back with you."

In a flash they'd left behind the Monkey King's towering palace, the mountain forests, and entered a gentler landscape of rivers and farm lands, rising gradually to a misty plateau. In the distance, high mountains rose up from the mist. Temples dotted the summit of one, much like the Jolly Buddha temple on Tai Shan mountain he'd visited with Mei. Crane Maiden landed in the courtyard of the largest building. Moments later her sisters joined her, and the children jumped from the birds' backs.

The place was deserted. White Tiger entered the poorly lit temple. To his horror, a huge painted Buddha statue lay face down on the ground, the altar bare apart from a few scattered lotus flowers and upturned vessels. He called out, but the only response was a cold silence that engulfed everything in the building. He returned to the courtyard. Smoke plumed skywards from incense burners, so White Tiger knew that whatever had happened was recent.

"Hey, guys, help me search the other buildings!" he commanded.

He and Rosie concentrated on those lower down the slope, including the monks' living quarters, whilst Amy and Andy combed the smaller temples and large dining hall higher up. They found only upturned tables and chairs, but soup in a large tureen still steamed.

"Makes no sense!" White Tiger puzzled after they met up again near the smouldering incense sticks. "Where on earth is everyone?"

"Tried the toilets?" suggested Andy.

"Those stinky huts over there? Um ... now why would *anyone* want to do that, ay? That's *really* dumb!" protested Amy.

The girl muttered on about keeping away from Andy for good if he were to go anywhere near the toilets. The three cranes set about preening themselves as she, White Tiger and Rosie stared at their friend approaching the toilets, one hand over his nose. He pushed at a door ... empty ... and another ... also empty ... but the third door remained firmly shut. There was a gap between the bottom of the door and the ground sufficient for a skinny limbo dancer to come and go at leisure. In that space Andy spied a couple of feet wearing sandals.

"You lot were so put off by the smell you missed the toilet feet!" he called back to the others.

"*Toilet* feet? He's raving!" mumbled Amy.

Andy knocked on the door. A voice muttered something in Mandarin.

"Hey! A toilet with feet that talks in Chinese!" Andy informed his friends.

Crane Maiden stopped pecking at her feathers and hopped across to the talking toilet. White Tiger followed, but the girls held back.

"Ask the toilet what's happening," White Tiger told Crane Maiden.

The crane talked in Mandarin, the toilet jabbered back, and the door opened. Out stepped a boy dressed in a white robe, his head shaved and bleeding.

"Says he's Yip Weishan, a postulant monk," explained Crane Maiden.

"What's that?"

"A boy who one day wants to become a monk. *Proper* monks wear yellow."

"Oh!"

Amy stared at the Chinese boy as if she'd seen a ghost. She tore a strip of material from the hem of her long dress, ran to him and gently dabbed his bleeding scalp with it. Andy looked worried.

"You've just ruined your dress!" he pointed out, but Amy

ignored him. Meanwhile, Yip, remarkably calm, spoke again to Crane Maiden.

"Everyone's escaped to the woods," continued the bird. "When the *wuya* birds came they kept diving and pecking at the monks who scattered in all directions. They threatened to gouge out the men's eyes if they didn't say where the Jade Snake was hidden."

Yip held the fragment of Amy's dress to his scalp whilst conversing in Mandarin with Crane Maiden. Every now and then she nodded.

"Inside the painted Buddha statue!" explained the bird. "They made the strongest monks push the statue off the altar and there it was on a string of pearls … the Jade Snake!"

The boy monk revealed more:

"He says the snake is the most beautiful jade work you could imagine. No one had set eyes on it for hundreds of years. Afterwards the *wuya* birds broke their promise and started attacking the monks' eyes. The others fled, but Yip hid in the toilet. Wants to protect the temple."

"Oh, poor Yip!" Amy exclaimed, placing a comforting arm round the young monk. Andy scowled. "I *must* take care of him! He needs …"

"When?" interrupted White Tiger. "How long's he been in there?"

Crane Maiden and Yip exchanged more words as Andy glowered, daggers drawn, at the monk. If he had a lance he'd have charged at him full tilt!

"Just before you shouted out in the language we're now speaking in, White Tiger," added Crane Maiden.

"Like … only minutes ago? They can't have gone far! For heaven's sake … what are we doing wasting time?"

"Wait … we must think this one out," cautioned Crane Maiden. "I took the straightest route here from the palace and saw no *wuya* birds on the way."

"Could've hidden in the forest."

"They'd have had no time to go and hide the speed we were going."

"So?"

"Must've taken another route. Using the river, I guess. Monkey King's idea, probably. They'll follow the river towards the horizon of the rising sun as far as the tributary that flows down from the monkeys' mountain forest. Then turn northwards to the palace."

"Chase them! You're a lot faster. We'll catch them up, destroy the Jade Snake and fly on to the palace."

"We'd never be able to destroy the Jade Snake! And there are eight of them against three of us. One could easily escape with the snake and we'd have lost time."

White Tiger felt hope slipping from his grasp.

"Reinforcements?" suggested Andy, looking at Amy for a response to his knightly wisdom.

"Where from?"

"I could go back and fetch King Arthur and his …"

"Good stuff, Andy!" agreed White Tiger. "But we'd do better calling for White Crane and Blue Dragon."

"That's only two more. King Arthur's got … "

"Four of *us* as well. And …"

"Five! Yip's coming too, aren't you?" Amy said, smiling

brightly at the boy monk. Without having a clue what she'd just said, Yip smiled back

"No monks!" objected Andy. "Draw a line at monks. They're pacifist, anyway!"

"Be quiet!" White Tiger felt dangerously close to losing his cool with his best legionary. "Crane Maiden, will you fly me and my friends ...?"

"*Absolutely* no monks," persisted Andy. "They don't make friends easily. And they're too spiritual!"

"He's only a postulant one," insisted Amy. "That's different."

"No it's not. Like caterpillars have to turn into butterflies, one day all postulants must turn into monks. They take vows, you know. Women are a no-no!"

"Poppycock!"

Yip beamed at Amy, still pressing the torn-off piece of dress to his head.

"Anyway, I don't care. He's still coming with us! Needs my attention, don't you, Yip?" Yip blinked. "That means 'yes'!"

"Amy's right," agreed White Tiger. "Can't leave him here, alone. He's only a kid. Anyway, Mei told me some monks in China are ace fighters. Kung fu and that. Shaolin monks are real experts. Might be one of them!" Andy glanced nervously at the Chinese boy. "As I was saying, Crane Maiden, you three better drop us off at the foot of Monkey Palace Mountain. Then get help as quickly as you can from White Crane, Blue Dragon ... and ..."

White Tiger's face betrayed his annoyance about something.

"Why hasn't *he* appeared yet?" he asked.

"King Arthur? 'Cos we've not dug him out! I keep telling you ..."

"No! Mr Qilin, as Mei called him. That mystical lucky creature. Appears to important people at time of need. What's he doing, for heaven's sake?"

It occurred to White Tiger that perhaps Mei, not he, was that important person. There again, this being the case why hadn't the Qilin rescued her when she emerged from the dragon noodle with her captors?

"Oh, forget him!" he continued. "Probably too busy looking for a lady Qilin. Okay, Crane Maiden, this is what we'll do. You and your sisters drop us off at the foot of Monkey King's mountain. We'll find somewhere we can hide safely from monkeys with spears and such whilst you lot fly off for reinforcements. White Crane, Blue Dragon and his missus, Red Phoenix ... even Black Tortoise if you can persuade him."

"He's a score to settle with you, White Tiger," warned Crane Maiden.

"Good fighter, though! Anyone ... *every*one you can get hold of! We've gotta stop Monkey King from putting the Jade Snake round Mei's neck. Nothing else matters! Got it?"

"I'll go with Amy," suggested Andy. "We're a great team. See how we found the Roman tablet together. Wouldn't have got far without that, would we?"

"No way!" objected Amy. "I'm not letting Yip out of my sight! He needs feminine attention."

Yip hadn't stopped grinning.

"Okay! You're with Rosie, Andy. See you all at the bottom of Monkey Palace Mountain."

White Tiger mounted Crane Maiden. Andy, cursing all monks and monkeys, climbed onto one of her sisters together with a jubilant Rosie whilst Amy settled herself on the back of the third bird, her arms about the waist of the boy monk seated in front.

"I'll make you a hat if you like. To wear till your hair grows again," she told Yip, gently stroking his bruised head. "It'll help your terrible wounds. I bet you were brave when you fought off those birds! By the way, why *are* you bald?"

Yip understood not one word although seemed totally at ease in Amy's company.

"Oh, didn't he tell you, Amy? Monks' girlfriends have to clean out temple toilets for the rest of their lives!" Andy called out after he and Rosie were lifted into the air.

"Shut up! Hope you fall off!"

"Why *do* you let her be so mean to you?" Rosie asked Andy as they soared down from the mountain, breaking through the cloud below to see a river snaking eastwards. "Stand up for yourself!"

The three cranes banked to the left and took the more direct route to the monkey forest.

"Yeah! Well, when I get myself a lance that pustular monk will be the first to enjoy the sharp end of it!"

Rosie sighed.

Soon, they were skimming over the tree-capped tops of massive, sheer-sided rock columns protruding from Monkey Forest. Some of the deep, intervening valleys were enshrouded in mist, and the scenery resembled that of the sage painting at Mei's house, but there was one thing White Tiger felt certain about: that there *were* no wise people in this forest apart from Mei, now a prisoner in that terrifying palace. When he spotted

Monkey King Mountain from afar he was overcome with dread that the Jade Snake was already around her neck and she'd no longer know him, enslaved forever to the monkeys.

"Please God, whatever happens to her don't let them turn her into a monkey!" he whispered. "As long as she still looks like my princess there has to be some hope!"

He prayed the wind might take his words if not to God then to Lord Buddha. But deep down he knew whatever help he might get from whatever source, divine or otherwise, it was up to him, as White Tiger, to save Mei.

The cranes now flew low between the mountains, dipping into the mist to avoid being seen. They touched ground beside Monkey King Mountain, a vast pillar of rock over a hundred metres across at its base and which vanished into the cloud above. Dozens of ropes dangled against the rock face.

"They can't all clear a thousand *li* in one leap like their King, so most monkey warriors use ropes," explained Crane Maiden. "Look! There's a space the other side of that big bush you can use as a shelter. Hide there till we return, White Tiger, and please *don't* do anything stupid. We know how desperate you are but if you try to get to the princess on your own, whether or not she's wearing the Jade Snake, it'd be suicide. And beware! This forest is full of monkeys."

They watched with apprehension as the three cranes soared up into the mist and vanished, wondering whether they'd ever see the birds again let alone their parents and school friends in Peebles.

"Right, guys, military discipline from now on? *Capisci?* ... as they say in gangster movies!"

45

White Tiger was determined to stamp out indiscipline in his army.

"Never watch them," said Amy. "Mum won't let me. She says …"

"Legionaries, Roman or Chinese, must be focused and alert at all times," interrupted White Tiger. "Respect each other!" He looked meaningfully at Amy and Andy. "And help fellow legionaries at times of need. One dead legionary reduces our chances of success by …" He did some quick mental arithmetic. "By twenty percent!"

"Twenty-five," corrected Andy.

"Twenty!" insisted White Tiger. "Yip's one of us!"

Andy groaned. Yip grinned.

"S'pose I *could* use him as target practice for …"

"Okay, our temporary camp's behind this bush," continued White Tiger. "And everyone keep eyes and ears open. Any sign of *wuya* birds and I'm up one of those ropes whatever Crane Maiden said. Better to die trying rather than let Mei get turned into the Monkey Queen."

"Oh, I'm not so sure …" began Amy, but White Tiger had already disappeared into the camp. The others followed. They discovered a rocky recess ample for four high school kids and a postulant monk. It was partly obscured by an overhang and a tangle of scrubby, scratchy bushes. Amy insisted on staying with Yip to protect his head (she feared any more scrapes on his scalp might prove life-threatening) and the boy smiled all the more as she fussed over him.

Using a sharp flint, Andy fashioned a lance from a straight branch and spent time sharpening the end till it was as pointy as a penknife. Rosie helped him, whilst White Tiger made repeated forays in the forest to look for water and food. Water was easy – there was a fast-flowing stream nearby – but food would prove a problem unless reinforcements were to arrive soon. All the time the boy was haunted by a terrifying image, the reason why he could not keep still for a minute: a mental picture of Mei's sweet face slowly turning into that of a monkey.

CHAPTER 4: MONKEY KING'S PALACE

Yip even slept with a smile on his face. Whether or not this had anything to do with Amy kneeling beside him, repeatedly stroking his bald head, White Tiger couldn't work out. He'd dismissed thoughts of the boy being simple, for there was a twinkle in his eyes that told him otherwise. Andy lay snoozing on his Yipwards-pointing lance, and Rosie was curled up beside him, snoring. Amy soon drifted off. White Tiger gave up on guard duty and slipped into a nightmare from hell:

Mei, now the Monkey Queen with a crown of pearls and a necklace dangling a live snake, was teasing and taunting him.

"Come with me, Mei," he begged. "We'll get you turned back into a girl. You can live with your parents again and I'll destroy the dragon noodle forever. Never again will you be scared of the Monkey King!"

"Scared of my husband? What *are* you saying you stupid little human? How high can you jump, ay? Two feet? Three at the most? Well, my wonderful husband can clear a thousand *li* ... that's three hundred miles by your reckoning. He could fight all of you off with his eyes closed. Why should I be interested in *you* with a monkey like that to take care of me? Be off with you before I call my guards to turn you lot into a bunch of *gui*. I'll count to ten ... and that's being a lot kinder than you deserve, White Tiger!"

Mei cackled like a witch as snakes emerged from the walls of the palace and slid towards him and his legionaries.

"Oh ... I forgot to say," added Mei the Monkey Queen. "There *is* no way out. Not for you! Still, I'll start counting anyway. Good luck!"

This dream faded to another in which he and Mei, now the girl he knew so well, were running as fast as humanly possible from a horde of monkeys waving spears. Arrows zinged past them until Mei screamed and fell to the ground. An arrow was sticking from her back, and when he turned her over her eyes had gone blank. There was nothing there. Dead eyes ... not Mei's! Monkeys were dancing circles round him whilst he knelt trying to stop her body from being snatched away. A large, mean monkey in a yellow suit, wearing a crown, grabbed him by the shoulders and began shaking him as if he was a toy rattle.

White Tiger awoke with a start. Andy was shaking him by the shoulders.

"Rosie saw it first," he said.

"What?" asked White Tiger, rubbing his eyes.

"One of those muckle black *wuya* birds."

Startled, White Tiger leapt to his feet.

"OUCH!" he yelped on banging his head against an overhanging rock. "Where? When?"

"SHHH! I thought you were on guard duty," whispered Andy.

"Never mind. Where ...?"

Andy held a finger to his lips and pointed at something dark on the ground outside their camp. In the dim light a few yards away White Tiger saw the shadowy form of a black bird the size of a turkey. It hopped about in the clearing, periodically stopping and cocking its head from one side to the other, as birds do, obviously looking for something ... or someone.

"Curses!" whispered White Tiger. "Either it's arrived ahead of the others or it's on look-out duty." He remembered his nightmares. "No time to wait for reinforcements! Curse the Jade Emperor! Letting us down big time, he is! Mei, at least! I'm going up one of those ropes. No idea where they lead to but ... but it's Mei's only chance!"

"You heard what the crane said! You're as good as a corpse the moment you start climbing. Wait, Stevie! They could be back any minute."

"I'm not *Stevie* here! And I don't *have* a minute! I'll creep round the bottom of Monkey King Mountain when the bird's facing the other way. You can distract it by chucking a stone. I'll find a way into the palace, and ..."

"Stevie?"

White Tiger turned his face away. Legionaries should *never* allow others to see their fear!

"Wait. I'm coming with you. I'll get my lance."

Back in their hideout the girls still slept, but Yip was awake, smiling as usual, with Andy's lance in his hands. Andy edged forwards cautiously, his hand outstretched. If the other boy knew kung fu, was also keen on Amy and had his only weapon then he, Andy, was dead meat!

"*I* go with White Tiger. You stay. Look after girls," said Yip in perfect English, handing over the lance. "Wait till cranes return."

"But ...?" Andy, puzzled but relieved, took his weapon. Besides, the idea of 'looking after' the girls appealed. "You just spoke English. Do you realise? Did you understand what we've been saying all along?"

He'd said some pretty rude things about the postulant monk! To his relief, Yip shook his head.

"Jade Emperor's messenger teach me when asleep. In dream."

"This place is so flipping weird! Okay, I'll stand guard whilst you go after Tarzan and watch him make a fool of himself. Maybe he'll listen to *you* now you can speak English."

"White Tiger not fool! Jade Emperor's messenger no help fool!"

"Help? By teaching you English in a dream? Huh!"

Andy returned to the camp entrance. Both the *wuya* bird and White Tiger were gone.

"Go on, Yip! Better get up one of those ropes quick! I don't need a dead friend. He's our leader ... *and* a good guy!"

Yip flipped his robe about his waist, ran at the cliff and leapt onto a rope. Gripping this between his feet, he pulled himself up, up, up ... and vanished into the low-lying mist.

"Thank God Amy didn't see that," Andy muttered.

"See what?" queried a girly voice behind him.

Andy turned to see Amy sitting up, stretching.

"Um ... the *wuya* bird. Pretty scary. White Tiger and Yip are climbing the ropes. Couldn't wait."

"Yip? You *let* him? With his terrible injuries? You're so horrid!"

Andy sighed. He sensed the girl wouldn't be the slightest bit concerned if *he'd* been injured, not even if half-pecked to death with both legs broken into a thousand fragments.

"I'm to look after you girls," he added, aware this was a job that scored zero hero-rating with the fairer sex. "Yip said."

"You don't speak Chinese!"

"He didn't *use* Chinese. Speaks English now, worst luck!"

"Yip? English? Wow! I can tell him I ... um ... you know ... explain how I feel and all!"

"Water?" suggested Andy. "I'll fill my trainer at the stream there and get my girl chum a shoe-full of fresh mountain water."

Amy glanced at his feet.

"You're wearing sandals! Anyway, your feet are stinky. Look can't you and Yip swop round?"

"Too late!" Andy replied, turning to face the mountain. "They could both be dead by now."

* * * * *

White Tiger almost let go of his rope from shock on seeing the boy monk's face appear through the mist only a few arm-lengths to his left.

"You speak English?"

Swinging against the cliff face, Yip told White Tiger about his dream. An old man with a beard, who called himself the Jade Emperor's messenger, came to the temple to take him to a hall full of people with calligraphy brushes working away at scrolls. He told Yip it was his destiny to help brave White Tiger and his army rescue Princess Hua-Mei and that he'd have to learn a strange language of the West. All night Yip knelt on the floor in front of a squat table memorising the language called English and when he awoke it was still there in his head.

53

"Cool!"

The boy's presence boosted White Tiger's flagging confidence as together, despite Yip's misgiving, they scaled the dangling ropes, praying to different deities they'd not encounter monkeys coming in the opposite direction. Soon they emerged above the cloud. The mountain soared heavenwards into the blue firmament, magnificent and terrifying, for somewhere up there Mei was being held prisoner. White Tiger refused to believe she'd already been turned into the Monkey Queen of his nightmare but the urgency of her need for him seemed all the more acute and he doubled his speed up the rope. Yip had no difficulty keeping pace.

They soon reached a protruding ledge. When White Tiger kicked away from the rock-face, he saw, looming above this, the grey stone wall of the palace. They were nearly there. His knees scraped against the craggy rocks and bled, but he continued to inch his way up. Yip arrived at the top ahead of him and reached down to help him up the last few feet.

"You need some of Amy's dress!" the monk joked, pointing at White Tiger's lacerated knees. White Tiger imagined the poor girl ending up with only her underwear on.

"Oh, it's nothing! Look, d'you think there's a door into the palace? I don't fancy facing those monkeys on the turret!"

He stood scanning the battlements of a turret high above them, from which dangled more ropes. From the air he'd already seen the turrets crawling with monkey warriors. Although he and Yip were in shadow with the sun hitting the opposite side of the palace, their white clothes would still render them easily visible.

White Tiger felt pretty exposed as he followed Yip along the rocky ledge keeping close to the palace wall. The vertical face of the mountain disappeared into cloud below, somewhere underneath which Andy and the girls would be crouched in their hideout awaiting reinforcements. He felt furious with the cranes for taking so long. Unforgivable … unless … no! He refused to consider the 'unless' involving the birds being shot down by arrows, leaving the five of them alone against a legion of fierce, armed monkeys, *wuya* birds and other enemy allies … not to mention the Monkey King. As for the Jade Snake, he prayed and prayed Mei wasn't already wearing the accursed thing.

Yip halted at the corner of the building, turned and touched a finger to his lips to warn White Tiger to stay quiet. Together they peered cautiously round at the ledge beyond … and at another *wuya* bird.

Head to one side, it hopped away from them, clearly expecting someone. When it turned and hopped back, White Tiger's jaw dropped. Dangling from the creature's vicious beak was a string of bright pearls at the end of which hung something greenish-blue, long and curvy. As the bird came closer he saw it more clearly: a beautifully carved jade snake with staring eyes, an open fanged mouth and a body and tail decorated with finely fashioned scales. Catching the light, it glowed green whilst swinging in response to the bird's hops.

"So wonderful!" whispered Yip in admiration, but White Tiger could feel only hatred for the ancient being or force that had created the object. He wanted to push past Yip and get to the bird so he could wring its neck and throw the necklace off the cliff to certain oblivion, but the young monk barred his way.

"No!" he said quietly. "See that door? Bird wait for monkey to collect Jade Snake. Monkey no fly. We follow monkey. Together overpower!"

They didn't have to wait long. The door creaked open and a helmeted monkey head appeared in the open doorway. The *wuya* bird stood between the boys and the large beast, no more than six feet away, its back to them. The monkey, wearing brown armour and carrying a heavy sword, slunk out onto the ledge. It gabbled something incomprehensible to the bird. Whether Mandarin or monkey-speak, White Tiger had no idea, but of one thing he was certain: here was a creature not even Yip with his kung fu could overpower.

It was his only chance. He ducked under Yip's arm and dived forwards to rugby-tackle the bird, but his arms closed around empty air and his face slammed the rock. Next thing, the monkey soldier lifted him by the scruff of the neck and suspended him over the precipice. He felt sick, not helped by the monkey's foul breath. It was almost a relief when the monkey let go. White Tiger could now die without that awful stink in his nostrils, but the saddest thing, as he sailed earthwards through the cloud, was that Mei would never know how hard he'd tried to save her from a fate worse than death.

* * * * *

"What's that noise?" Rosie asked.

Andy and Amy were sitting beside the hideout entrance. Andy raised his hand to warn Rosie to remain silent. They, too, had heard a rustling in the undergrowth.

To Andy's relief, a large white bird with red and black bits on its head and neck broke through the scrub into the clearing, followed by another and another. A fourth bird, completely white, also appeared. Behind this crane, a dark shadow lurked in the bushes.

"What kept you?" Andy asked Crane Maiden. "And who's that?"

He jerked a thumb at the fourth bird.

"*That* is none other than *Bai He* ... White Crane, in your funny language!" replied White Crane. "I do hope you're not as bad as White Tiger! You know, but for Pretty Flower I'd have dropped him off over the Great Wall last time. I'd do anything for her, though! Where *is* White Tiger, by the way? They told me he was leading our army."

"Got fed up waiting. Climbed one of those ropes with Yip the pustular monk."

"Postulant! He's dead cool too! Never once complained about life-threatening injuries on his head," said Amy.

"Hmmm! Amy tore off half her dress for him to cover a scratch the size of a flea bite!"

"It was *not*! He nearly bled to death!"

"Oh Buddha!" moaned White Crane. "He's *worse* than White Tiger! And where on earth are Blue Dragon and his wife, Red Phoenix?"

"Blue Dragon's coming!" explained Crane Maiden. "He's so excited at the thought of seeing Pretty Flower again he keeps darting off in the wrong direction. Red Phoenix is always looking for him. He's fast, but has no sense of direction, see."

White Crane squinted at the dark shadow in the bushes.

"Why did you have to go and call on Black Tortoise? I'd

rather hold a tea ceremony with a pack of hungry lions than have *him* in our army!"

"Don't be so hard on the guy!" rebuked Crane Maiden. "He's got a tough job as guardian of the North. Terrible winters. Hordes of uncivilised barbarians. Enough to make any tortoise grumpy. Besides, those monkey fighters are no match for Black Tortoise. He's part snake as well, you know."

"Snake!" echoed White Crane. "Yeah, and *this* is all about the Jade Snake, right? We're wasting our time if Monkey King's already put it round Pretty Flower's neck. She'll be his forever. And slowly turning into a Monkey Queen! Such a lovely child, too. Prettiest girl in Hangzhou, they say, and that's quite something."

"And Amy's the prettiest girl at our school in Peebles," insisted Andy. "Say hello to Amy!"

"Hello, Amy! But ... oh, who are *you*?"

White Crane stepped into the hideout to take a closer look at Rosie. He'd never before seen a girl with red hair and he seemed transfixed by her. Rosie, who'd scowled on hearing Andy's remark about Amy, appeared embarrassed as the crane stared open-beaked.

"*I'm* just Rosie," she replied. "Not important! Dunno why I'm here really. I suppose I hoped ..."

She glanced at Andy and blushed.

"Not important? But of all the immortals I've ever seen, *you* are the most beautiful!"

The girl turned an even deeper shade of crimson. Was he making fun of her like those horrid children at primary school when she had a boil on her nose?

"I'm not immortal!" she answered. "And if you're being ..."

She was interrupted by a terrific crash. Everyone rushed to the clearing to witness trees being snapped like trampled flower stalks, accompanied by breathing as loud and deep as the rumble of a heavy truck. An enormous blue head appeared above the broken branches. The head swivelled and fixed an unblinking disc-like eye on the little group.

"WHERE'S WHITE TIGER?" roared Blue Dragon.

Both Amy and Rosie clung to Andy who stood pointing his lance at the dragon's head. All three backed away when the beast stepped over a tree, filling the clearing but for his long twisting tail which trailed away into the forest.

"It's ... um ... like this ... er ... White Tiger's ... um ... gone. Aye, he's ... er ... gone and ... um ... well, sort of gone ... like," faltered Andy.

"GONE?" bellowed Blue Dragon. A rush of moist, stale air escaped from his gigantic mouth, throwing the children backwards. Andy's lance shook like a road-drill in his trembling hand.

* * * * *

As White Tiger fell through the cloud he expected his whole life to flash past him. He'd read somewhere that this is what happens moments before death, but all he felt was anger with himself for letting Mei down. He closed his eyes for one last mental look at her face before his body would be dashed to smithereens on the ground below. When it happened, the landing was surprisingly soft and feathery. Was he already floating on a puffy cloud in heaven, he wondered? Would Mei be there as well? But why was he now moving so fast in the reverse direction?

Wow, some cloud!

He opened his eyes. Trees and rock-face flashed past as he shot upwards. He was clinging on to what felt like feathers. He looked down. Red feathers! He looked ahead ... a long horn, like that of a unicorn. The creature turned its large lion head to face him.

"How's that for quick service?" the Qilin ('Chee-lin') asked.

"Quick? Better late than never, I s'pose. Thought I was dead for a moment," replied White Tiger tetchily. "What kept you so long?"

"Time of *need*, White Tiger! Remember? I was beginning to wonder whether you'd *ever* need me again!"

"It's Mei who needed you! I was trying to get the Jade Snake from that *wuya* bird when I fell and got chucked off the edge by a blinking monkey. It's over, Qilin! Don't you get it?"

"Over? Oh no! And it's *you* the princess needs, not me!"

The Qilin spiralled round Monkey King Mountain until they were high above the palace. Circling, White Tiger looked down and saw a commotion on one of the turrets. Little monkey figures ran about, some tumbling over the edge into the cloud.

"Lower please. Down there! I wanna see what's happening," he urged the Qilin.

Wings spread, the Qilin glided down towards the palace turret where, on closer inspection, White Tiger saw Yip felling and flinging monkey warriors in all directions. On spotting the enormous approaching creature, the few remaining simians fled, screaming, through a door at the side of the turret. The strange animal, lion-faced, eagle-bodied and dragon-tailed, landed beside Yip. White Tiger slipped from its back and the boy monk, unfazed, smiled.

"Should have listened to me!" he remarked. "This is your Qilin, right?"

White Tiger nodded.

"Where did that bird go? We've gotta get the Jade Snake before ..." he began, but Yip cut him short:

"Wait! Yip hear monkey talk when he take snake. Princess now dance for King and other monkeys in Great Hall. He'll put necklace on her when dancing. 'Monkey King's revenge', monkey soldier say."

"Of course! Mei tricked him with her dancing to get the magical pearl and golden staff back for the dragon. He's gonna do the same thing. Whilst she's distracted he'll ... no, I can't bear it!"

"When dance finished she's his! Must hurry. Follow me!"

"But the others? And our reinforcements?" asked White Tiger.

"Qilin! Here!" Yip called out.

The Qilin, who'd been licking his feathers as a cat licks its fur, looked up.

"Me?"

"A clearing at bottom of mountain. In a hideout behind a large bush. Three kids. Friend called Andy. A co-legionary. And two girls. Both pretty. Maybe some cranes, Blue Dragon ..." explained Yip.

"Old misery boots?"

"Married now!" said White Tiger. "That *must've* cheered him up a bit. Whatever, please get help! And hurry!"

The Qilin took off as White Tiger and Yip left the turret via the same doorway through which the monkeys had fled, ascending, in darkness, a narrow, spiral staircase that opened onto a vast hall. The door to the hall was hidden behind a large silk screen decorated with a picture of mountains, streams, flowers and monkeys. One of the monkeys in the hall was twice the size of the others and wore a gold crown. The boys crouched behind the screen and listened to the excited monkey jabber and to something else, so very different … the haunting sound of the *erhu*.

Whenever Mei danced for Stevie in her home it would be to strains of an *erhu*, a two-stringed instrument as typically Chinese as bag-pipes are Scottish, and its sound reminded him of their time together. His anger swelled as he crouched beside Yip wondering whether Mei was there on the other side of the screen and already on her way to becoming the Monkey Queen.

* * * * *

Andy scrambled to his feet and pointed his lance at the dragon's enormous eye.

"AND WHAT MAKES YOU THINK I NEED A TOOTHPICK?"

"Please not so loud, Blue Dragon. You'll scare the girls!" reprimanded Crane Maiden.

"Oh, so sorry, girls! The boy offered me a toothpick. I worried there was something wrong with my breath. Might put Red Phoenix off. Couldn't face a divorce. Not so soon! In fact …"

Toothpick?

Andy, his pride damaged, lowered his lance.

"White Tiger and the boy monk couldn't wait," explained Crane Maiden. "They've gone on ahead. Don't stand a chance

against a huge army of monkeys, not to mention the King himself ... the fiercest warrior in the land!"

"Isn't!" called a gruff voice in the forest beyond the clearing.

Andy braved Blue Dragon's smelly breath and left the hideout and the cowering girls to investigate. A large upright black tortoise with a snake's head and swords dangling from his shell emerged from the trees.

"Thinks he is, but isn't!" repeated Black Tortoise. "Lend me your golden staff, Blue Dragon, and I'll knock the Monkey King to the far end of the land. Red Phoenix will love you better if you help rescue the princess."

"I'll ... um ... think about it!"

Blue Dragon lowered his head and his great eyelids snapped shut as he tried to think. Andy now realized the delay hadn't entirely been the cranes' fault.

"No time!" urged Crane Maiden.

"Humour him! He's a liability if he gets the grumps!" White Crane said. "Oh, do let's go!" he added impatiently. "I'll take one of the girls. Prefer girls. They argue less. Lighter, too. Perhaps ... um ... the one with red hair?"

"Okay," agreed Crane Maiden. "My sisters will take the other two and I'll go on ahead. Monkey King won't suspect me. I could offer myself for a painting. Crane paintings bring luck for important people, you know. I'll pretend I've heard the princess is to become the Monkey Queen and see if I can persuade him to make a painting of me to bring them luck. I'll say ..."

Blue Dragon flicked open an eye and shook his head, showering Andy with dragon saliva. Something was protruding from the tip of his nose.

"Girls! Quick! One of you pull that arrow from the dragon's nose," urged Crane Maiden. "The rest of you guys watch the bushes!"

Andy, lance at the ready, approached the bushes nearest the dragon's head. Rosie ran to remove the arrow from the beast's nose, and Black Tortoise whisked out two swords. A dozen monkeys appeared, armed with spears and swords, their weapons raised high. A whirl of slashing black fury descended on them as Black Tortoise went into action. In the blink of an eye a dozen monkey corpses littered the clearing but further fierce monkey warriors soon replaced them. Andy joined the fray, dodging the simians, stabbing with his lance, parrying their spear-thrusts.

If only I had a horse and decent armour, the boy thought, glancing back to check the girls were watching. Water trickled from Blue Dragon's eyes and Rosie was stroking his nose where the arrow had been. Amy was hidden from view by Crane Maiden and Andy decided he actually preferred to look at Rosie anyway.

There seemed no end to monkeys emerging from the forest. Some, unarmed, ran at Andy and tried to bite him. He ended up dropping the lance and kicking and punching instead and he'd lost count of the number killed by Black Tortoise.

What a warrior that guy is! King Arthur would've knighted him, you bet! Wish I could be ...

"RAAARGH!"

Blue Dragon rose to his full height, snapped his great jaws at the monkeys and in a flash they were gone. Andy didn't dare ask why he'd not done that in the first place. The girls and all but one black and red-headed crane had vanished. He ran to the bird and scrambled onto its back

"Hold the fort," he called out to Black Tortoise who looked somewhat put out that the Blue Dragon had got rid of the monkeys so easily. "Wait ... Crane! Just a minute!"

He slipped from the bird and ran back for his lance. On returning to remount the crane there was burst of colour above. A large, multicoloured, lion-headed creature landed beside the Blue Dragon, curled in its wings and strutted towards him.

"Are you White Tiger's army?" the Qilin asked.

"And are you by any chance something to do with White Tiger and the princess?" Andy queried. His friend had made mention of a colourful mythical beast made up from different animal parts. It was called a 'cheese bin' or something.

"White Tiger's Qilin!" came the reply.

"Aye, I guess I am. His army, I mean. Man, this gets weirder and weirder! Why couldn't Stevie have got himself a normal girlfriend, ay? What with that Black Tortoise guy and the muckle Blue Dragon ... and now you turn up! Oh well, I guess the girls have gone on ahead! On other birds. They're sort of army too."

"Yeah! Saw White Crane and two of the crane sisters! Wondered what *they* were doing round these parts. Okay, just follow me."

Andy remounted the crane.

"This way, big guy," he called out to Blue Dragon.

Leaving behind Black Tortoise to ponder over how *he* fitted into the scheme of things, Blue Dragon, Qilin and Andy on a crane shot up towards Monkey King Palace. On breaking above the cloud, Andy spotted three large white birds circling high in the dazzling sunlight.

* * * * *

The music stopped.

"Silence, everyone!"

White Tiger hoped he'd never again hear the voice of the Monkey King! He and Yip froze statue-still. Even taking a breath felt risky.

"Is the *erhu* player doing his job to your satisfaction, my dearest? This is to be the most important dance of your new life, you realise! Are you ready?"

White Tiger clenched his teeth. How dare that monkey call Mei 'my dearest'! Cautiously he shuffled sideways, flat against the screen, and peered from the edge with one eye.

Mei stood alone in the centre of the hall, her back to him, on a large carpet. She wore the same red dance dress with long sleeves she had on when they were last in China together. It only just fitted, for she had grown. Her feet were bare. The Monkey King lounged back on an ornately-gilded throne, his evil face fixed on the girl. Two brightly dressed monkeys stood on either side of the throne, keeping their King cool with large fans. In orderly rows, along each of the other three walls of the hall, armed monkey warriors stood to attention. From the corner of his eye White Tiger glimpsed a wizened old man with a straggly white beard, no more than six feet away, seated on a stool and holding a bow against an instrument that resembled a miniature skinny cello with a long neck. He'd never before seen an *erhu*. It seemed odd that a slender, insignificant-looking thing could produce music evoking such powerful feelings in him.

He wished Mei would turn round, catch his eye, and flee with him to the turret, leaving Yip to fight off warriors single-handed with his kung fu. But were they too late? Was she already wearing the Jade Snake?

He looked again at the Monkey King. Thank God, the snake was in the monster's hands! The monkey began playing with it, slipping the string of pearls between his hairy brown fingers.

"Speak, my child!"

"Yes, my Lord!"

Mei's voice sounded so sweet ... better than any music ... but 'my Lord'? Coming from Mei? She *hated* monkeys! Had the Monkey King so destroyed her spirit she would obey him when the time came?

The music started up again and Mei danced. The beauty of the music was perfectly matched by the beauty of the girl. As she danced, making ever-changing, circular patterns with her sleeves, first to one side, then the other, the boy could not take his eyes off her. And when she turned, head tilted, her long hair half-covering her face, he wanted to run up and flick the hair away so he could see her properly. Then her back was to him and he wished the music would never stop. If it went on forever perhaps nothing terrible could happen to her.

After a series of graceful genuflexions Mei twirled again. Her face, now uncovered, was once more towards him. Their eyes met. Lovelier than ever, she stopped dancing, staring as if she'd seen a ghost. Her eyes lit up and she ran forwards, shrieking:

"STEVIE! STEVIE! WHITE TIGER! *PLEASE* SAVE ME!"

White Tiger broke cover, but they never reached each other. One of the nearest monkeys threw a net over the girl, and she

fell to the floor, caught like a fish. Another hurled a spear at White Tiger, but, as if by magic, Yip was at his side and caught the spear, flicked it round and used it with devastating effect against the swarm of monkeys now surrounding the boys. The Monkey King strode over to the struggling girl, picked up the net and held her dangling whilst he cut at the mesh with a knife. Lowering her down, he pulled her free from the net and slipped the Jade Snake around her neck.

"TAKE IT OFF, MEI, TAKE IT OFF!" yelled White Tiger, frantically kicking out at sword-swinging monkeys to get to her, but either she'd lost the will to resist or no longer had ears for him, for she stopped struggling and seemed perfectly happy for the Monkey King to lead her by the hand to a door at the far end of the hall. They halted and the King, laughing, turned and bellowed:

"TOO LATE, WHITE TIGER! THE PRINCESS IS MINE! DID YOU LIKE THE NET? YOU SHOULD HAVE! YOUR IDEA! REMEMBER?"

Mei and the Monkey King disappeared through the door. The King's echoing laughter faded to nothing. Moments later a stream of chattering monkeys emerged from the same door and spread out across the hall. White Tiger picked up the spear of a felled monkey warrior and he and Yip stood back-to-back as the enemy closed in on them in a shrinking circle of flailing weapons and snarling teeth. He never stopped to think why they didn't kill him quickly with a spear through the heart or an arrow through the brain; instead he struck out when close enough to see the red streaks in the whites of their eyes. One grabbed his spear and yanked it away. He no longer felt Yip's back against him. Alone, he faced death.

CHAPTER 5: MONKEY PRINCESS

"Wow!" exclaimed Andy when Blue Dragon shot past him, slamming into the palace turret with bullet precision. Monkeys and fragments of stone showered from the building into the cloud below as the dragon, perched precariously on the roof, ripped at the walls, opening up a hole into the uppermost floor. The cranes above stopped circling and sped downwards, aiming for the hole.

"Hold tight!" advised Andy's mount before straightening her long neck and entering the palace like a bolt from a cross bow. Inside the Great Hall she slowed, gliding to and fro, as did the other cranes, dodging spears and arrows. Amy and Rosie, terrified, clutched onto their birds for dear life.

Yip, completely surrounded, was fighting off monkeys single-handed. He caught their hurled weapons as if playing a game of catch, returning them to senders with deadly accuracy.

"Watch this!" Andy called out to the girls. "Knights to the rescue! It's called tilting!"

He pointed his lance at one of the monkeys closest to Yip.

"At 'em, girl!" he yelled, digging his heels into the side of the bird. Shrieking "EUREKA!" he flew at the monkey target. More and more simians fell to his lance, and soon a gap opened up before Yip. Andy held up a clenched fist for Amy's benefit, but the girl was too busy worrying about Yip to notice. Then all four cranes began to dive at the monkeys, pecking away and driving them insane.

Monkeys tried to regroup below the hole in the ceiling. The Great Hall went dim. The simians peered up, each ugly face a picture of fear, for filling the hole, baring his enormous teeth, the vast blue head of the Blue Dragon grinned down at them. A cloud emerged from his mouth blanketing screaming monkeys in mist. Andy dismounted and called out to Amy and Rosie. The other birds appeared from the mist and landed beside the boy. He helped Amy off her crane, his speech prepared in his head and ready for delivery:

Will you now attach your hanky to my lance, oh fair damsel?

But before he could utter a word Amy ran to Yip, flung her arms around the postulant monk and kissed him on the cheek.

"Let me nurse your wounds, you poor, poor thing!" she said. "Oh ... why didn't you say you could speak English? I've so much to tell you!"

Yip smiled happily.

"Don't know why I bother!" mumbled Andy, deflated as a burst balloon.

"You were great!" assured Rosie, slipping down from White Crane.

"I'd go along with *her* if I were you," added White Crane. "However irritating I find you, if *she* says you're great then you're great! Do you realise this girl with red hair is the most ravishing female human I've ..."

"WHERE'S WHITE TIGER?" boomed a voice through the mist.

Silence! Slowly the mist cleared and revealed the Blue Dragon, the size of a double-decker bus, his huge, fierce eyes fixed on a trembling monkey, the only remaining live simian.

"Yes, where *is* he?" Andy asked Yip. "You were supposed to protect him!"

"Hang on!" objected Amy. "How can you blame Yip? He was fighting off hundreds of monkeys before Blue Dragon rescued him!"

Blue Dragon? What about me, for heaven's sake?

"White Tiger fight bravely! But when Yip turn round gone," explained the boy monk.

"There you are!" said Amy. "Gone! Both Stevie and Maisie! Can we clear off home now? And take Yip with us? He could start up a martial arts school in Peebles. I'll help him. Become his secretary. Every busy man needs a secretary, you know."

Andy frowned. Leave his friend behind? No way. Even if Stevie were dead, he'd bring the body back. That's what good legionaries do. Knights as well. He was certain they used to bring bodies back from the Holy Land during the crusades and bury them with full military honours. He could do that for Stevie later when they got back to Peebles. At the church service he'd be up there in the pulpit telling the congregation (which would include Amy!) how he'd bravely tried to save his leader's life when ...

"I ask *erhu* player!" suggested Yip, interrupting Andy's train of thought. "Ask about White Tiger!"

Andy scowled as Yip broke free from Amy's loving embrace and approached the old man who sat stiff, yet serene, with his instrument between his legs, the bow still against its paired strings. The boy monk spoke quickly in Mandarin and the musician replied slowly, pausing periodically, rocking himself forwards and backwards in un-played rhythm. Yip said a few more words, the musician nodded, and the boy returned.

"Taken prisoner," he explained to Andy and the girls. "Mean one thing, say *erhu* player. White Tiger's destiny not to die. Not yet!"

"And Maisie ... the princess?" queried Andy, thinking about the purpose behind their military expedition to ancient China.

"She too has destiny. Maybe to become Monkey Queen."

"Told you we're wasting our time!" moaned Amy.

"We are *not*! And didn't you notice how brave Andy was?" responded Rosie stamping her foot.

Andy felt better, but why couldn't those words have come from Amy's sweet lips?

"Andy, *you're* the leader now. What should we do?" Rosie's eyes searched the boy's face for an answer.

Mmmm, me the leader, ay? he thought. *Perhaps she is pretty.*

"So?" the red-haired girl continued.

Yeah ... actually, she's very pretty!

"No question! We've gotta find White Tiger. *Our* destiny!" he announced.

Rosie gave him such a loving smile it almost melted his insides. He looked from Rosie to Amy, wondering.

Wow! She really is prettier than Amy. Like White Crane said ... she is ravishing!

He high-fived with Yip whose puzzled expression revealed the boy had no idea why they should slap hands together.

"Only one way out from here," the boy monk said. "Where Monkey King take princess before Blue Dragon arrive."

He pointed to the door at the far end of the hall.

"Okay, guys. Follow me," commanded Andy. "Birds stay here! Help Blue Dragon guard our monkey prisoner. He'd never fit through that doorway, anyway!"

Holding his lance in front of him, with Yip behind, Amy hanging on to the boy monk's white robe and Rosie at the rear, Andy crept through the door, down the steps to the floor below.

"Amazing!" he exclaimed.

They beheld a magnificent banqueting hall, the top table laid out for two. Monkey King and Monkey Queen, perhaps? Delicious smells wafted from the adjacent kitchen and tantalised the children's nostrils. Strangely, the banqueting hall and kitchen were deserted.

"Oh, I'm starving. Can't we eat first?" asked Amy. For once Rosie did not disagree with her. Andy, not wishing to face mutiny so soon into his leadership, followed the girls into the kitchen. A feast fit for royalty was spread across the tables, the food still hot.

"Didn't think you liked Chinese," Rosie said as Amy tried dish after dish.

"This is different!" replied Amy through a mouth full of stir-fried beef with *pak choi*. "Better here in China, any day! Maisie's always saying so."

Andy helped himself to his favourites ... chicken and cashew nuts, spare ribs and special fried rice.

"What's this?" he asked, picking up a flask and sniffing the open top.

"No!" advised Yip. " Only for feast!"

But Andy had already raised the flask to his lips and gulped down most of the contents.

"Wow! Miles better than Irn Bru!" he exclaimed, handing the near empty flask to Yip before hiccupping.

"Ugh! Rice wine!"

Andy burped and wondered why he was holding two lances in the other hand.

"Hurry girlsh! Musht find White Tiger!"

"Andy!" Rosie called out when she saw the boy sway towards the stairs. "What's the matter with you?"

"Demote him!" suggested Amy. "Yip can be our leader from now on!"

"Shut up! I'm sticking with Andy."

Squabbling like free-range chickens, the girls followed Yip and Andy down to the next floor where they discovered a magnificently spacious bedroom and sitting room, numerous ante-rooms and a balcony looking out at the pointy mountains of Monkey Forest. Doubtless the King's own suite! Below were two floors of smaller bedrooms and living quarters, probably for important monkeys; beneath these, over two levels, squalid quarters for unimportant monkeys.

"Shhhh!"

Yip silenced the bickering girls as they began the descent to the lowermost floor and the dungeons.

Andy, still trying to work out which of the two lances to use in battle, followed the postulant monk. He halted when the other boy held up his hand … or were there two Yips and two hands? Yip darted forwards, disappearing through a dark doorway. Andy poked with his lance at the stubbornly solid wall a few times before finding the open doorway. He turned and grinned at the two Amys behind him.

"Doorway'sh not where it's sh-shupposhed to be," he announced.

"Quiet!" she whispered. "You heard our leader!"

"No, no! Knightsh in armour *have* to lead. Anyway, maybe not!"

"Maybe not what?"

"Maybe not Amy'sh hanky on my ... hic! ... lanshe!"

Amy sighed her exasperation. There was a gasp and a thud from the darkness ahead, followed by a girl's scream.

"What's he doing?" queried Rosie.

Yip reappeared.

"Come!" he said. "*You* speak to princess!"

Andy staggered on through the doorway then stopped. The girls passed by and easily stepped over the body of the monkey jailer felled by Yip, but Andy's lack of balance made this a challenging exercise. He tripped and fell on top of the monkey. Rosie turned to help him back onto his multiple feet.

"This way," said Yip, leading them along a dark passage lined by tiny barred prison cells. Each contained a thin, bedraggled monkey peering sadly out. They reached the last, somewhat larger cage. Here a lovely, long-haired Chinese girl, wearing a red dress, sat cross-legged on the floor. Around her neck was a string of pearls at the end of which hung the Jade Snake, and she looked scared out of her wits.

"So beautiful!"

"The shnake or the girl?" asked Andy. He'd always agreed with Stevie that Maisie was beautiful but he didn't think his friend would appreciate the boy monk talking like that about his girl. He'd have to put his foot down.

"The Jade Snake!"

Andy breathed a sigh of relief. He knew he was in no fit state to defend his friend's honour however many lances he had in his hand.

"All my life I hear about Jade Snake and its powers. Now to see so close! Amazing!"

"Yeah, but what about the girl ... hic! Maishie? The prinshesh? What do we do?"

Yip shook his head.

"Too late. See!"

As Maisie looked blankly ahead, tears streamed down her cheeks. When Andy and the girls stood in front of her she showed no response. There wasn't even a flicker of recognition.

"Does she still speak English?" asked Rosie, her eyes moistening. "She looks so lost, the poor thing."

Yip shrugged his shoulders.

"Maybe unhappy because Monkey King's gone. I ask."

He spoke to Maisie in Mandarin. She nodded, but said nothing. Yip said something else and she nodded again, the flow of tears increasing. She began to sob. Finally she spoke in between sobs.

Yip turned to the others.

"She say she's Monkey Princess. Princess Hua-Mei now dead. Wait for master to return to make immortal. Only then can be happy again."

"Let's break in. Release her," suggested Rosie. "Take that thing from round her neck. Perhaps we could ..."

Yip shook his head.

"No! Princess would die! Cannot undo curse of Jade Snake!" the boy informed her. "She say Monkey King go with White Tiger to demand Lord Buddha make monkey and princess immortal in return for life of White Tiger. Princess say she dance forever for her husband."

"Husband?" Andy queried, angered. "She's only a kid! I'll kill that fiflthy monkey!"

"No!" replied Yip. "Princess would die as well if you kill. Monkey princess cannot live without her lord."

"Then ... we'll take her hosh ... er ... *hos*tage. Demand he return White Tiger in exchange. At least we get Sht ... Sht ... *Stev*ie back!"

"Can't! Monkey Princess say her Lord take key for cage with him. Also Yip think White Tiger not want to return without his princess."

"Houston, we have a problem!"

"Uh?"

"Sorry. What they radioed to NASA base from Apollo 13. Made into a movie, it was! Ashtronauts ... no ... um *astro*nauts going to the moon hit a glitch. Thought they'd be shtuck up there. I mean sht-sht ... oh ... never mind! So what now?"

"Monkey King take White Tiger to Holy Mountain. Meet Buddha."

Did the word 'Buddha' cause a slight change in the Chinese girl's eyes? Brighten her blank expression? Andy wondered.

He tried to keep Maisie in focus. The knowledge that he

and the girls could be stuck in ancient China for the rest of their lives was having a sobering effect. The rice wine still rendered everything blurry, but at least he was now certain there *was* only one girl sitting alone in the cage. So the prison was to keep others away from Maisie rather than to keep her locked up, for it seemed she'd lost all common sense and now thought of herself as a monkey despite her human beauty.

"We leave the princess here, then? Return to your temple?" Andy asked Yip.

"No! Monkey King take White Tiger to *different* temple on most holy of five holy mountains of China. Tai Shan! Near where Blue Dragon lives."

"*That* weirdo? Still, at least he speaks English. So we go there ... and then what? Wait for Buddha to promise he'll make the Monkey King and Maisie ... the Monkey Princess ... whatever ... immortal? After that can we all go home? Without Maisie? Back to square one?"

"Lord Buddha cannot make Monkey King immortal. Only suggest he take different path."

"Don't understand!"

"Few can! But there is still hope for princess. You wait outside now," suggested Yip.

"Like three thousand feet up flapping my hands like a naff bird?"

"Follow Yip!"

At the other end of the dungeon, Yip opened a door and showed Andy and girls the rocky ledge where he and White Tiger had spotted the thieving *wuya* bird carrying the Jade

Snake. The girls, who'd stopped squabbling after seeing their monkey-worshipping friend alone in a cage (*shock*, Andy reckoned!), gasped in horror. Amy began screaming (*fear of heights*, Andy reckoned!), so Yip took her back with him to the Great Hall to fetch the cranes (*part of the pustular monk's plan to keep Amy for himself*, Andy reckoned!). Rosie and Andy sat outside together, backs to the palace wall, to await the arrival of incoming flights for Tai Shan.

Yeah! White Crane has a point? Andy thought, squinting at Rosie.

"What are you staring at?" the girl asked.

"Wondering what you'd look like with yellow hair," the boy replied. "Like Amy's. Na! Think I prefer red."

"Boring old Red-Nosed Rosie, ay?"

Andy didn't know what to say. The rice wine had muddled up his mind and he couldn't think clearly enough to deal with females.

"I wouldn't say boring. Or red-nosed. Actually ..."

Rosie burst into tears.

Hurry up cranes, he said to himself, feeling hopelessly out of his depth. How could he tell Rosie he fancied her when he was in love with Amy? Perhaps he should become one of those Mormons with multiple wives Stevie once told him about. There again, not much fun being surrounded by a swarm of weeping women.

"She's so *mean* to you. It's not fair! What've I done wrong? Tell me!"

Tell her? A real live damsel in distress? There's no escape now, laddie! But what should I tell her?

The more Andy looked at the weeping girl the more he considered there was nothing whatsoever wrong with her and an awful lot wrong about Amy.

"I could organise a divorce," he suggested.

"Between Maisie and the Monkey King?" Rosie wiped her eyes. "They're not married yet. She's too young."

"No! Me and Amy. She's only a girl 'chum'. Not even a girl *friend*. I haven't attached her hanky to my lance ... and she does nothing but drool over the pustular monk."

Rosie giggled.

"*Postulant*! Pustular means covered in pimples."

"Like I said ... pustular! Postulant's not a yukky enough word. Anyway, I've grounds for a divorce even if I *am* madly in love with her. Well ... perhaps not actually in love."

Andy tapped his lance on against the rock. The point had become scrunched over by battle. He'd have to find another flint somewhere to sharpen it.

"Do you still have your hanky?" he asked.

Rosie screamed.

Maybe I should have second thoughts about females in general, full stop! Andy wondered.

"Look ... honest ... um, please don't get emotional," he begged. "I only wanted to ... you know ... like I'd be honoured if ... er ..."

"No! Over there!"

Rosie pointed up at the sky. Something large and red was coming towards them ... and fast!

"Right ... well!"

Andy stood and held his lance skywards. If the thing turned

out to be a violent red dragon, rather than a dozy blue dragon, he'd show it what a knight's lance could do. Toothpick indeed! As for Rosie, he felt an overwhelming desire to impress her with courage way beyond anything those celluloid Hollywood heroes were capable of.

Not a dragon, but a huge crimson bird!

"It's okay, Rosie. No need to scream anymore. Only a bird!"

Wings outspread, and the size of a small aircraft, it brought to Andy's mind a picture book he got hooked on as a kid … about the Red Baron, a crazy German First World War pilot. How he'd once longed he could have been the RAF guy who shot down the Red Baron!

Any closer and you're a dead duck! he thought as the bird got nearer.

He glanced over his shoulder to make sure Rosie was looking.

CHAPTER 6: NO BIG DEAL

Wake up Stevie ... wake up, for God's sake!

Over and over, White Tiger repeated the words to himself ... just in case the whole thing had been one of those strange dreams he and Maisie sometimes shared. Nothing happened. The net was squashing his nose and his knees dug into his chest like those of a supermarket chicken as they soared heavenwards, hung for a moment, then fell a few hundred miles to Earth, only to repeat the exercise time and time again. He'd have vomited if in the correct position, but vomiting upright seemed a bad idea. He tried thinking of other things to take his mind off puke-tinged thoughts ...

NASA?

He and Andy often talked about space travel. Bouncing up and down, each bounce a few hundred miles, reminded him of Space Rockets. Should he promise the Monkey King a job with NASA – if he were to survive – in exchange for Mei?

Oh my God, where is she now? How can our friendship survive the Jade Snake?

He saw her face so clearly, begging him to save her. Now she was cursed forever because he'd failed her! If only they hadn't wasted precious hours in that police station being bombarded with stupid questions!

A sudden jolt and the whizzing up and down stopped! His bottom hit rock as the Monkey King flung him carelessly to the ground but he refused to let the pain get the better of him.

"Enjoying your own medicine, White Tiger? Remember the little journey you and the princess had me do last year, ay?"

The boy blinked at the Monkey King's ugly features looming down at him.

"Didn't believe me when I said your pretty little friend would pay for her thieving trickery, did you?"

"Trickery? She was only getting Blue Dragon's magical pearl and golden staff back for him to help the farmers with their crops! You're worse than a thief! You're a ..."

White Tiger struggled to think of a word to describe anything evil enough to transform a twelve year old girl into a monkey just because she wanted to help people.

"Yes, White Tiger, but things have changed since then. She's the best dancer in China ... and so lovely, too! Soon I'll be her attentive husband. You'll never need to worry about her again. She'll get all she wants ... and more!"

"She *wants* to get home to her parents!"

"No longer! She wants her future husband back. LOOK!"

The Monkey King stooped down, removed something from his pocket and held out a brown hairy hand inches from White Tiger's netted face. An oval of white jade with decorated edges lay snuggled in his palm, but it was what the boy saw in the centre of jade that hit him like a punch from Muckle Mikey back in Peebles: Mei still wearing her red dance dress, alone on the stone dungeon floor, her long, black hair straggled about her gorgeous face, not brushed sleek as she knew he liked it, and she was speaking softly to herself. He recognised the language for it was the one she spoke at home to her parents – Mandarin – but he understood not one word. He felt cross with her for not teaching him more ... for not ensuring he'd be as fluent in *her* language as she was in his.

"Shall I translate for you, little foreigner?"

So that's all he was now ... a foreigner in a strange land, separated from Mei who no longer had reason to remain friends with him. Should he hate *her*, too? Would that ease the pain of what the monkey was about to tell him?

"She's weeping for me to return. Telling me all the time how she misses her Lord and how she promises to make him happy forever after with her dancing. She talks of the patterns she'll make with her arms to describe the leaps of the Monkey King. She even says ..."

"SHUT UP!" yelled White Tiger, unable to raise his trapped hands to cover his ears.

"She has no memory of you, now, Little Tiger of the West!" goaded the monkey. "And if Lord Buddha sees sense ... if he gives the great Monkey King and his future queen what they both desire – immortality – I may allow you to go home if you promise never to return."

Why? If Mei's lost to me forever why should he still fear me?

Uncertainty stirred White Tiger's courage.

"Kill me instead!" he demanded. "So Mei remains mortal and dies as well. And doesn't have to put up with your ..." He couldn't think of the word he wanted to say ... the stinky breath word. *Helli ... or halli-something?*

Monkey King impatiently grabbed the net and dragged the boy over the gravel and into a cool, dark place. The sweet, heady smell of incense calmed White Tiger's anger and soothed the pain of his grazes and bruises.

"I do no deals, Monkey King! Your destiny is your own," boomed a deep voice ... one that had seemed so gentle, so full of hope, the last time he met Lord Buddha. Now that same voice appeared to offer nothing. No eternal life, no release from torment ... no death.

But why did Lord Buddha reply to Monkey King in English? So he, White Tiger would understand? Understand *what?*

"Lord Buddha ... to achieve immortality, on your command I went to the far end of the world and back again, but you tricked me!" complained the monkey.

"I trick no one. You *thought* you were at the end of the world because you wanted to be there. If you seek immortality what stops you from just thinking it?"

White Tiger had pins and needles in his feet and wished the talking would stop so he could be released to shake his legs and get rid of the invisible, pointy bits prickling him.

"Lord Buddha, you wouldn't deny the princess immortality when she did so much for you last year, would you?"

Quit the prattle and let me free, begged White Tiger's mind.

Monkey King, prostrate before the Buddha, remained unaware when he began to roll sideways.

"I need nothing and the princess did nothing for me. She merely fulfilled her destiny," continued the Buddha. "Why won't you listen to what I say and seek *yours,* Monkey King? Find a true path! Immortality leads nowhere!"

White Tiger rolled on unnoticed ... ground, door, painted ceiling, flash of shiny gold, upside-down monkey, floor, door ...

"But Buddha, see how she longs for me to return to her!"

The Monkey King held up the oval jade into the gaze of the Golden Jolly Buddha statue. The boy stopped rolling and listened.

"How can you truly love the child when she took from you those things you so desire?"

Hey, Mr Statue, whose side are you on? questioned White Tiger.

He continued to roll. Ceiling, Buddha, upside down Monkey King kow-towing to the statue, floor, door. He halted again when the monkey replied:

"Listen to her, Lord Buddha! She loves *me* now! Would you prevent her from becoming the great immortal Monkey Queen? Deny her wish to dance for all eternity for the one she loves?"

"*Her* wish or the wish of the Jade Snake?"

At last! thought White Tiger.

"Jade Snake? Oh, but Lord Buddha ... that little trinket she wears? How on earth could you think it has any influence over her?"

"*Prove* your love for the princess, show me her destiny is also yours and you and she will live on together forever, in Monkey King Palace!"

White Tiger rolled out of the temple and slammed into a rock face. Suppressing the urge to squeal with pain, he began rubbing himself up and down against a jaggy projection until the mesh of the net had torn sufficiently for him to free first one, then the other arm, before stepping out of it. The talking in the temple had stopped. White Tiger flung the net over the side of the mountain and sneaked behind a rock. On discovering he'd escaped, Monkey King ran from the temple.

"White Tiger, hear me!" he beckoned. "I've no need for you now. No deals, Lord Buddha says. Only have to prove my love for the Monkey Princess! Easy! Give her what she wants, huh? Me! Ha ha ha! She wants *me* now! So go home. Don't come back. No one needs you here! You'll never belong in China! You ..."

Without Mei at his side to give him a gentle, calming down pinch, White Tiger flipped. He scrambled out from behind the rock, his cover blown, to confront the Monkey King.

"Your love for Mei?" he challenged. "It's a lie! She made a fool of you and you only ever wanted revenge! You don't wish to make *her* immortal either. Only yourself! Then you're gonna kill her, aren't you?"

The Monkey King held a long staff. Not the Blue Dragon's, thank God, but nonetheless a fearsome weapon.

"Kill her? Oh, you've got it so very wrong, little friend! Like I said! You don't belong here and you don't understand. So the princess can *never* be yours."

"I don't want to *own* her!" answered White Tiger, fuming. "We're just friends. Anyway, last time the Jade Emperor sent for *both* of us. *That* makes me belong here."

"Jade Emperor? Pfff! Needs replacing, he does!"

The angry glint in Monkey King's eyes confirmed that mention of the Jade Emperor was similar to lighting a fuse. The monkey leapt at White Tiger, teeth gnashing, his staff whirling like a helicopter blade. White Tiger dodged the attack (rugby training proving to be of use at last?) and darted back behind the rock. He had two options, both fatal. Wait and face the Monkey King, or jump from the rock to the valley below. He jumped.

Mid-fall, something colourful came up to meet him, and instead of continuing down, he shot forwards. A large lion face turned to look at him.

"Time of need again?" queried the Qilin.

"Bit overdue ... but yeah! Hurry! Take me back to Mei. To the Princess. I dunno what that monkey plans to do, but whatever it is she's in dead trouble."

"Monkey King Palace? No, not yet! Yip told me to take you to Blue Dragon's cave and wait there."

"Have they got the princess? Rescued her?" White Tiger asked anxiously.

"That's the problem. Only Monkey King can release her from the cage in his dungeon."

"What about the Jade Snake? Has she taken it off?"

White Tiger's mind flashed back to the monkey's white jade stone in which a tiny image of Mei wept for her captor.

"She'd die. No mortal person should try," the Qilin replied.

A fate worse than death? Surely better Mei should die unchanged rather than live forever as the Monkey Queen, her mind gone?

It was a short journey to the Blue Dragon's cave, as White Tiger remembered from when he and Mei were last in ancient China. The place was deserted. The pool of dragon tears had long since dried out, but whilst White Tiger sat and waited, and as the Qilin cleaned himself, he thought back over the times he and his girlfriend had been together both in China and in the Scottish Borders, and he feared another pool might form. A pool of *human* tears! He'd happily drown in *that* pool.

The Qilin glanced up at him.

"Don't forget you're her Yang! *That's* your destiny and the Jade Snake can't change it!"

"Did you just read my mind, Qilin?"

White Tiger quickly brushed the back of his hand across his eyes.

"No need to!" came the reply. "Your mind's where I come from."

* * * * *

After gently landing on the rocky ledge, the huge red bird cocked her head to one side to get a better view of the Scots boy offering her a stick.

"No thanks. We birds don't have teeth! Mind you, my husband Blue Dragon could do with a toothpick. I keep telling him to look after those teeth of his. Wouldn't do for him to make 'smelly breath rain', ay?"

Andy stood, mouth agape, disappointed he'd lost another opportunity to impress a female.

"Are you Red Phoenix?" asked Rosie.

"I am," replied Red Phoenix, bowing respectfully.

"I like your red."

"I like yours, too, Rosie. Word's getting around, you know. White Crane's telling people."

"What 'word'?"

"About your red hair. And your beauty."

Rosie turned rose pink and tried to avoid eye contact when Andy winked at her.

"*She's* gonna attach her hanky to my lance," he informed Red Phoenix, though with his lance reduced to dragon toothpick category the chivalry of this seemed uncertain.

"Wait here, please," requested Red Phoenix. "The others will soon be along. I've gotta find my husband. Didn't see him shoot past, did you? He's in such an excitable mood he could be almost anywhere."

Rosie tried, but failed, to suppress a chuckle. Andy liked the way she giggled; more natural than Amy's laugh which anyway was usually directed against him.

Red Phoenix took off and disappeared round the corner of the palace. Moments later four white cranes flew up from below. They landed in perfect formation close to where Andy and Rosie sat. Yip and Amy, astride one bird, dismounted with the girl still clutching onto the young monk's arm as if he might vanish should she let go.

"We go to Buddha!" announced Yip.

"Okay guys! We're off to see the Buddha, the wonderful Buddha of Oz ..." Andy sang, but stopped the instant Rosie frowned at him. He couldn't afford to upset her as well. She still thought of him as their replacement leader till they found Stevie. He considered Amy a dead loss now she'd been 'stolen' by the pustular monk. Pity, he thought, for she had been his true love (*his* opinion, at least) for such a long time. A whole year, in fact!

"*I'm* going with Yip," Amy informed him, as if reading his mind. "I've been telling him all about girls' fashions in Peebles. He's really interested, you know. And I told him secretaries have to dress posh to create an image."

Andy wasn't sure whether the girl's covert declaration of love for the bald boy disappointed or pleased him.

"Well," he said. "As a matter of fact Rosie and I have a lot to discuss too!"

With exaggerated gallantry he helped Rosie onto White Crane before climbing up in front of her ... quickly sliding off when White Crane twisted round and gave him a threatening bird scowl. Its beak was dangerously close.

"*Behind* her, please!" White Crane said. "I want something worth looking at when I turn my head."

Rosie grinned. Andy agreed the bird had a point, but it seemed odd for him to have to put *his* arm about *her* waist. It wasn't that he didn't enjoy it. It was great, but he'd have to ask the girl her thoughts on women's lib some day. Also, there was still the issue of tying her hanky to his lance. He needed to show White Crane *he* was her knight. Losing a female to a pustular monk was one thing ... but to a toothless bird? No way!

"Rosie?"

"Uhuh?"

The girl turned her face.

Even better close up! Never been just inches from Amy's face. Perhaps, before our divorce, I should give it a try. For the sake of comparison!

"D'you think the Buddha will knight me for services to ... whatever?" he asked Rosie.

"Na! He'll be religious. Getting knighted's not a religious kinda thing."

"What about King Arthur and the Holy Grail? That was religious. So were the Templar knights during the crusades. They wore crosses on their breast plates."

"*I'll* do it!"

"What?"

"Knight you! My Grandpa has an old Japanese sword. From

his dad in the Second World War. He was victorious, you know."

"Cool! Wish I could be victorious."

"You were pretty brave fighting those monkeys. I watched you."

"Tell you what. I'll persuade Stevie back home to make you a princess like Maisie. *Then* you can knight me. Okay?"

Rosie grinned happily, and both seemed to forget they were soaring through the sky at an incredible speed. Ahead were the other three cranes, one bearing Yip and Amy, flying in Red Arrow formation.

"Are you all right back there, Sir Andrew?" Rosie asked.

"Fine, Princess Rosie! Did they cut off heads with it?"

"What?"

"The Japanese. With that sword."

"Oh! Dunno!"

Andy felt chuffed he'd one day get knighted with a sword that might have cut off heads. It somehow made him feel important.

"D'you still have your hanky?" he asked.

Rosie patted her dress sleeves. Nothing.

"Must've lost it." She didn't like to tell the boy it was Stevie's, anyway.

"Try ... you know!"

He tapped his chest. He'd watched movies in which women hid things close to their bosoms and Rosie already had a bit of a bosom. The girl felt inside the top of her dress and her face lit up. She pulled out the hanky and handed it to Andy.

"Wow! It's still got that dragon stuff stuck to it."

Three points of multicoloured light sparkled in a fold. Carefully, the boy tied Rosie's hanky round the end of his lance, ensuring the knot wouldn't come undone in the heat of battle.

"Rosie Brown, I hereby declare you to be my damsel."

Happiness shone from the girl's face as they continued their journey across ancient China.

* * * * *

A sound similar to that of a collapsing ten-storey building shook the ground. It was followed by a loud thud and an angry roar.

Buildings don't roar. Anyway, there are no buildings nearby, thought White Tiger. *An earthquake, perhaps? Oh Mei, I wish I'd asked you to tell me more about that earthquake you were in.*

A picture of Mei, trapped and pining for the Monkey King, refused to leave his mind. He'd hoped thinking about the same girl back home, Maisie Wu, would erase the image, but this only made him sadder. Like their friendship, Maisie Wu belonged to his past and the new Mei, even lovelier (if possible) in her distress, had wanted nothing to do with him.

'You don't belong here?' Is this what she now believes?

"His landings are terrible!" said the Qilin.

"Who? What are you talking about?"

White Tiger felt as if he was on a different planet ... one without the Mei he knew so well.

"Blue Dragon! Coming in to land! We all hoped marriage would help his landings but he's as clumsy as ever."

It went dark. A large blue head filled the cave entrance.

"Sorry I'm late. Just checking!" Blue Dragon said.

"Uh?"

"Checking on my Red Pearl and magical golden staff. I'd hidden them nearby. As soon as I heard Monkey King was coming to see Lord Buddha I thought I'd better check. You see, he'll want to impress Pretty Flower now he's got her forever."

"HE HAS NOT!" shouted White Tiger unable to contain his rage. "IT'LL NEVER HAPPEN! NEVER, NEVER, NEVER! I WON'T LET IT!"

White Tiger feared anger might burst open his body and leave little bits all over Blue Dragon's cave. He tried to calm down. He even felt angry with Mei for no longer being with him to soothe his nerves. Nothing calmed him better than a soft pinch and a giggle from the Chinese girl.

"Oh ... I just remembered the other reason I came," added Blue Dragon, fixing a plate-like eye on the boy.

"Spill it!"

Monkey King back in his palace? He and Mei married already?

"There's been an ... er ... accident."

White Tiger could only think of car accidents. Had one of his parents ... or Mei's ... been killed? Would Blue Dragon hear about it even here in ancient China? No longer could anything surprise him.

"White Crane. Hit a rock trying to dodge the *wuya* birds. You'd better come quick."

* * * * *

"What *was* that?" Rosie asked.

Something black flashed past her face, so close she felt a swish of air.

Andy turned. It darted over them, reappearing on the other

100

side. Not one, but two ... no, three ... more ... five ... six ... black objects.

"OW!' he yelped when one of the *wuya* birds dived at him and pecked his arm, but this remained firmly around Rosie's waist and he felt proud of himself for protecting her from the peck.

"Cover your face," he warned the girl. "They go for the eyes!"

"CAN'T!" shrieked Rosie. "I'M HOLDING ON TO THE ..."

White Crane banked, and for a moment Andy thought he and Rosie would fall to their deaths. He dug his heels into the bird's side. They righted. White Crane turned and zig-zagged, stabbing at the air with his long beak. Andy imagined he was on an airliner attacked by jet fighters. Over short distances the larger craft would have little manoeuvrability. Same thing in the naval battle against the Spanish Armada.

He saw their game. No match against the crane's long beak, the *wuya* birds were driving them back towards Monkey Mountain and into the cloud. Black shapes shot from the mist, bombarding Andy, Rosie and White Crane with painful stabs. Rosie was screaming, and Andy felt powerless to reassure her and stop the noise. He also screamed when, out of that ghostly grey mist the cliff face raced towards them. He raised his lance, taking aim at a protruding rock.

WHAM!

Wood hit stone. Still clutching the lance, he found himself jerked backwards horizontal. Next thing, he was vertical but upside down, clinging onto Rosie whose arms hugged White Crane's neck as if it was the Tree of Life. Suddenly his feet left the bird. The crane was doing a loop the loop. He was still vertical but the right way up, legs dangling and kicking air. Rosie, her long red hair smothering Andy's face, was now beyond screaming. Her hair smelt really good! Everything went strangely quiet as they veered to one side before bottoms hit crane again and Rosie's hair returned to her back.

Yeah! Definitely prefer red to yellow thought Andy just before the cliff face hurtled in their direction again. Another attack by the squadron of *wuya* birds distracted him, and his lance hit the cliff at an angle. White Crane's emergency avoidance failed, his wing struck rock and they spun out of control, dropping through the cloud like a stone. The ground rushed upwards as if gravity had gone into reverse. Moments before impact and certain death, in a blur of white, black and red, Crane Maiden was underneath them. They glided forwards, bird on bird, skilfully weaving between tree trunks till they came in to land in their hideout clearing now littered with dead monkeys.

Black Tortoise looked up.

"Told you the dragon should've given me his golden staff!" he grumbled.

Crane Maiden warned him to keep quiet or she'd scream in his ear. As Andy assisted a trembling Rosie off the injured White Crane, he wondered where Black Tortoise kept his ears.

"Oh, why did I agree to this mission?" moaned the distressed White Crane. "I'm sure my wing's broken. What use is a magical crane who can't fly? I'll lose my job with the eight immortals on Penglai, you bet!"

White Crane's right wing hung limp.

"I'm so sorry!" apologised Andy. "I did try fighting 'em off with my lance but we were hopelessly outnumbered."

"Lance?" queried Black Tortoise. "Magical, by any chance?"

"Well, it's got Rosie's hanky tied to it. That'll make it *special*, I guess!"

"No!" insisted Rosie. "It was *you* who were special, Andy! Don't do yourself down. It's all because of *her* you've no confidence and it's not fair! Oh ... talk of the devil!"

The other cranes came in to land, one bearing Amy and Yip. Amy jumped down and ran to Rosie and Andy.

"I ... I saw that," she said, visibly shaken. "You two okay?"

"As if you care!" snapped Rosie.

"I do! Don't be so rotten. I was Andy's friend long before you joined the legion. Remember? Muckle Mikey and Crazy Davy and ..."

"Leave off, Amy. Rosie nearly got killed."

"Just wanted to say how brave you were, Andy! That was so cool! I told Yip you're my boyfriend, and he's okay with it. Actually ..."

Frowning, Amy glanced back at the boy monk.

"Actually, all he does is smile. Doesn't say a word! I mean he's a great fighter and that, but when I tell him things, like how I put on a really short skirt and makeup, like a secretary, when I go out with my girlfriends ... if Dad's not around ... he doesn't seem to be listening. He only smiles."

Yip was now scoring mega-points in Andy's brain but Amy had him confused. He loved two women! Was that acceptable ... or was it acceptable? Thankfully, a disturbance of colour above gave him time to defer any decision-making.

A threesome of creatures, Blue Dragon, Red Phoenix and the weird beast called a Qilin, descended into the clearing. White Tiger rode the Qilin magnificently, Andy thought, but when he and his co-legionary were face to face he saw his friend was a broken man.

"Did you see the Buddha?" Andy asked.

"Sort of," came the flat reply. White Tiger remembered only the golden flash of the statue as he'd rolled himself out of the temple ... and the Buddha's un-reassuring words.

"So ... did they do a deal? Maisie becomes immortal and stays here as the Monkey Queen and *we* all get to go home."

A wave of panic hit Andy. He'd now *have* to choose between Rosie and Amy and he still couldn't decide. Amy had a point. He knew her a lot better. Rosie had changed, but she'd been pretty mean to Maisie on the Chinese girl's the first day at their last school.

White Tiger shook his head.

"I dunno! If Monkey King can prove his love for Mei she's his forever. A dancing slave! If not, she dies like the rest of us. When the time comes. But ... oh Lord, that curse! She's *begging* for him to return to her! Her mind's gone."

"No!"

It was Yip. All turned to look at the postulant monk.

"Cannot take mind away. Buddha teach this," he said. "Only find right path to truth. Jade Snake change path for princess ... but other paths still there. Somewhere! If remove Jade Snake, she find true path again."

Her frown gone, Amy looked admiringly at the Chinese boy. White Tiger shrugged his shoulders wondering whether Mei's true path could ever now involve him.

"But we can't release her from the cage, and if we force her to take off the Jade Snake she'll die," he said.

"Cage no problem!" Yip insisted.

"Er ... excuse me, but aren't you forgetting something, dude?" asked Andy eager to keep Yip in his place. After all, he hadn't yet made up his mind between the two girls. "Like a key? Magical, maybe ... and probably only the Monkey King has one?"

"No problem for Blue Dragon," observed the boy monk, smiling at the great beast who beamed at Red Phoenix as if he'd just saved the world.

"You mean ...? But he could hurt her. She might ..." began White Tiger, but felt unable to complete his sentence. The word 'die' seemed too terrible to say out loud.

A fate worse than death?

Perhaps the same word offered Mei hope. To be hit by a lump of stone as the Blue Dragon smashed through the palace wall would perhaps be a welcome release for her.

"Easy! Consider it done," announced Blue Dragon, raising himself up to full height.

"I'll kill you if you hurt the princess!" Red Phoenix informed him.

White Tiger had taken little notice of Red Phoenix, although he'd heard many mythical stories about the dragon and the phoenix from Mei and her *Kung-Kung* (mother's father). If his thoughts hadn't been with Mei he might have been amused by the idea of a bird a quarter the size of the Blue Dragon trying to work out how to kill her husband.

"And then?" White Tiger asked.

They all looked at Yip.

"Penglai!" the Chinese boy said.

"Penglai?" queried White Tiger.

"Penglai?" echoed White Crane, anxiously.

"Where's that?" asked Andy. He wasn't sure he was ready for more flying about.

"Where I work!" replied White Crane. "With a broken wing I expect the eight immortals living there will fire me."

"That's why *you* have to go too," insisted Yip. "The immortal healer will fix your wing and ..."

He glanced at White Tiger.

"And Mei?" the other boy queried.

Yip nodded.

"Worth a try!"

"Kill two birds with one stone?" offered Andy, pleased with his humour, but it went down like a lead balloon, except for Rosie who tried to overcome an embarrassed snigger.

"Not funny!" grumped White Crane. "So what if I *am* a bird, huh? I'll forgive you this time, Mr Andy, because of what you did up there, but I could easily go off you."

"Right!" exclaimed White Tiger, a glimmer of hope sparking renewed authority in his tone. "Me, Qilin, Blue Dragon and Red Phoenix rescue the princess, come back for White Crane ... then, um ... to Penglai. Know the way?" he asked Qilin.

"Never been there. I'm *your* Qilin. Ask *him*."

He flicked his dragon tail in White Crane's direction.

"Can't fly!"

"*I'll* take you," announced Blue Dragon.

"No you won't! Enough scares for one day! Have to draw a line somewhere," insisted White Crane.

"Red Phoenix?" suggested White Tiger. White Crane nodded. "Andy, you stay with the girls. Yip and Black Tortoise will look after you."

"Hey, Stevie! You never saw me in battle. Tell him, Rosie! *I* don't need looking after, do I?"

His eyes sought support from both girls, his chest pouting with pride. Rosie was about to say something, when Amy piped up:

"Andy was dead cool. I saw it all. Like pushing White Crane away from the mountain. Protecting the bird, he was."

"And *me!*" mumbled Rosie.

Amy caught sight of Yip smiling again. At *her*, perhaps? Maybe the boy monk was only playing shy when she'd tried to explain mini-skirts to him.

"So is Yip. Cool, I mean. *And* he speaks Chinese," she added.

Rosie groaned. Andy, now less sure of his position with the females in his life, recommended Yip go with White Tiger and Mei to Penglai, but in the end the young monk remained with Andy and the girls (*his* choice). Shortly, the 'Princess Hua-Mei Rescue Team', as Andy called the little entourage, took off, White Tiger in the lead riding the Qilin.

They easily identified the corner of the palace where Mei lay hidden in her prison mourning separation from her beloved monkey 'husband'. Red Phoenix and Qilin held back, hovering high above the mountain, White Tiger praying Blue Dragon could punch a hole into the dungeon without sending the entire building crashing to the valley below. He closed his eyes as the great beast flew at the palace like an airborne blue bulldozer. On re-opening them he was amazed to see an accurately placed hole just wide enough for him to crawl through.

Mei *should be okay,* he thought.

The Qilin landed him on the jutting ledge and the boy eased himself through the hole into Mei's prison cage, so dark after the brightness of the sun that at first he saw nothing. He called out:

"Mei? Maisie? You here?"

Silence!

He crept blindly into the cage fearful he might tread on the girl and harm her.

"Maisie? It's okay. I can take you home now. We'll forget all about monkeys. Their King can't prove what doesn't exist, so you *can't* be his forever. I heard the Buddha myself. And they'll fix the Jade Snake in Penglai. Yip said."

Nothing! His eyes were slowly adjusting to the low light. He made out the bars … and the cage door was open.

"MEI!" he yelled, his voice muffled by the damp, stone walls. "MEI! MEI! PRINCESS!"

The cage was empty. It felt as if invisible jaws had opened up and swallowed him whole, leaving behind a ghost to shout the girl's name over and over. As he approached the door his foot kicked something on the ground, sending it skidding. He looked down and picked up Mei's yellow notebook with a red flower on the cover.

She had my notebook with her! How come? Smuggled it from Peebles when they snatched her away, though her clothes were left behind?

The notebook gave White Tiger heart. Did the Jade Snake truly have the power to force the girl to forget him and love the Monkey King, or had she been pretending when he saw her weeping in the monkey's hand? Had she left it behind on purpose, knowing he'd come back for her ... or (his worst fear) had the Monkey King found it hidden in her clothing and discarded it to make sure she had nothing left to remind her of her life in Peebles or of him?

White Tiger slipped the notebook into his pocket and checked out the other dungeon cages. Deserted! No Mei, no monkeys! He ran up the stairs calling out, searching every level. Finding his girlfriend's notebook had flicked a switch, turning despair into anger. Anything vaguely monkey-like would have been torn apart by his fury, but he appeared to be the only living thing in the palace.

He returned to the ledge outside.

"The Monkey King's taken her already," he announced.

"Where?" asked Blue Dragon. The beast was spoiling for a fight with the Monkey King. After all, Pretty Flower *was* his favourite human!

White Tiger shrugged his shoulders.

"Only know he's gotta prove his love for her to become immortal. *Both* of them, that is! But I don't believe him. He's using her to become immortal himself. He hates her."

"Pretty Flower? Impossible! No one could hate her. Not even a monkey."

"She tricked him last year."

"That's nothing! He lives by trickery."

"So ... you're saying ...?"

If the Monkey King really loved Mei it made a big difference, for perhaps the hideous creature *would* be able to prove it.

"Could be," replied Blue Dragon.

"Only one thing for it! Get the others and go look for them. Everywhere! We'll split up. Search the whole world. I'll never give up."

"I'm with you on that!" agreed Qilin.

"Of course you would be!" said Red Phoenix. "You *come* from White Tiger! We've gotta be more sensible. Have a plan, or Monkey King's always gonna be one step ahead. You'd never catch him. Never get the princess back!"

"I tell you, I *know* what he'll be after. He'll think he can impress her with ..." began Blue Dragon.

"Oh, be quiet, husband!" interrupted Red Phoenix. "You do witter on so!"

As they flew down to the clearing, White Tiger hoped Mei's notebook might give them a clue, but when reunited with his friends it seemed of minor importance, only adding more uncertainty to the pervading glumness.

White Crane was wondering whether he'd ever be able to return to his job ferrying the eight immortals to wherever they wanted to go. Amy couldn't make up her mind between daring Andy and brave Yip, upsetting Rosie who feared the love of *her* life would go for blonde if the chips were down. Andy was unsure. He agreed with White Crane. The red-haired girl *was* amazing, but there was the added problem of the 'pustular' monk. Would *both* girls soon be swooning over *him* if they were to remain in China for much longer?

All, however, agreed on one thing: although decisions

would be easier to make back in Peebles, no one was prepared to desert White Tiger.

White Tiger finally summoned up courage to show Mei's notebook to the boy monk, hoping he might be able to translate it. They sat in private, their backs to a tree, as White Tiger flipped through pages of Chinese writing ... hesitantly at first, for he felt he was prying into the girl's secrets and had no permission to do this.

He stopped and flicked back a few pages. Something had caught his eye. He found the page and blushed. Mei had drawn a large red heart, and inside, in neat round girly script, were the words: *I love White Tiger.*

Yip grinned.

"You understand our writing, too?" White Tiger asked, attempting to hide his embarrassment.

"No. Underneath heart writing in Chinese. Your destiny, I think!"

White Tiger had noticed the neat calligraphy underneath the heart.

"What's it say?" he asked, expecting total denial of the statement above it.

"Say ..." Yip paused, working out the correct English words. "Say wish White Tiger promise marry me one day. Um ..." Another pause. "Say no want go back China without White Tiger. If say marry me ask parents let me stay in Peebles."

White Tiger turned from crimson to something several shades darker. He knew girls thought about that sort of thing sooner than boys, but Mei and he were only twelve. Had their friendship really meant that much to her back in Peebles?

"Look through it," he said, handing the notebook to Yip. "Particularly the last few pages. She might've left a clue. Or ..."

Aye ... might confirm the worst! The curse of the Jade Snake in those beautifully written Chinese characters ... Mei declaring undying love for a monkey?

Yip translated aloud:

"'I wait for my Lord to return ...'" he began. "'I ... er ... become his queen and live forever ... I ... um ... I practice Monkey King dance all the time to remind me ...'"

"Anything else more helpful?" interrupted White Tiger, his heart sinking like a brick in a pond.

"Here!" announced Yip staring at the last page of Chinese writing. "'Now my lord will prove his love. Take me to a special place ...'"

The *monkey seems to have it worked out. If he really does love her she's lost. Me too!*

"A special place? Any clues where this might be? We've gotta stop him. It's her only chance!"

"Special place. Nothing more. Ends there."

White Tiger knew how vast China was. A million people could search the country for all eternity and never come remotely close to discovering an unidentified 'special' place. He'd tell the others and together they'd decide: whether to abandon Mei to the curse of the Jade Snake and return to Peebles whilst this still remained an option, or stay on in China, risking death or worse, in order to hunt for the Monkey King and his new princess.

"What about the Garden of the Queen Mother of the West?"

questioned the Qilin. "If he steals two magical peaches he and the princess will become immortal, Buddha or no Buddha."

"Unlikely. Ripened last year. Only happens once every sixteen thousand years. He's not gonna wait ... and Mei won't live that long, anyway."

"*I* think ..." began Blue Dragon.

"SHHHH!"

Red Phoenix silenced her husband with an angry glance.

"*I* think we should all go home," said Amy. "My parents will be spare. We're missing school and ..." She glanced warmly at Yip. She'd been thinking again about the martial arts class they might set up together in the evenings and at weekends. "Yip could come back with us. He won't want to return to the temple ... will you, Yip?"

Oh my God! thought Andy. *This is all I need!* He'd have to have *his* say on the matter.

"But ..." began the Blue Dragon before Andy could open his mouth.

"SHHHH! Let others speak, can't you?" snapped Red Phoenix.

The despondent dragon flopped his head to the floor and closed his eyes.

"I ... um ..." began Andy. He realised he needed to be careful with his choice of words. He knew the importance of words to women, and to lose Rosie as well to the pustular monk would be too much for any knight to bear. "I think Yip belongs here," he declared. "Anyway, he's a monk and monks must remain cerebrate."

"Celibate!" corrected Amy. "I'm sure monks don't have to

remain celibate in Peebles. I could find out for him, though. He *must* come back with us. He's my friend. He'll have a great life teaching martial arts. He already knows about girls' fashions ... and I bet he doesn't really fancy girls in these funny long dresses."

"Perhaps ..." began the Blue Dragon, cautiously opening an eyelid.

"Well, what about his vows?" Andy knew monks had to take all sorts of vows concerning the shaving of heads, vegetarian food ... and ... well, women, of course!

"He can vow ... um ... vow to teach his secretary all she needs to know. About life and stuff! He's very wise, ken. Or perhaps you didn't! Maybe Rosie's poisoned your mind against him."

"I've done *nothing* of the sort!" objected Rosie.

Blue Dragon lifted his head.

"No! Not 'perhaps'! Definitely! Like I've been trying to say. The mountain near Tai Shan where I use my red pearl and magical staff to bring on the rain. He'll try it himself. To impress the princess. Won't succeed, mind you. Because he's not a dragon. But he'll think he can. To prove his love to her. So ... no problem! We let him become a thief again. That's all!"

The dragon closed his eyes then sank to the floor to prove to Red Phoenix he wasn't trying to usurp her authority. White Tiger broke the stunned silence:

"You mean ... you're gonna let the Monkey King steal those things again ... so we could ambush him and the princess? On that mountain of yours? Can you be so certain?"

Blue Dragon said nothing, fearful he'd already overstepped

the mark with his wife, but Yip showed no hesitation in backing the dragon.

"Dragon right!" the boy monk said. "Monkey King love the princess in monkey way. Jade Snake cannot make princess bad. Only make her desire person ... or monkey ... who puts snake around her neck. Monkey must show he cares about people to impress Pretty Flower. If he makes rain for farmers ... for love of princess ... then might become immortal."

"Making rain clouds only works for dragons," mumbled Blue Dragon without raising his eyelids.

"Monkey King will try anything for princess," announced Yip. "We go to mountain!"

"*All* of us?" queried Amy. "Like you and me as well? Couldn't we ..."

"Need *every*one! Monkey King fears our army now. Means there will be many monkeys on Blue Dragon Mountain. See how they'd all left Monkey Palace."

"Not a monkey in sight!" agreed White Tiger.

"Finally! A *real* battle!" Andy announced with enthusiasm. "Be sure to look out for the lance with the hanky on it, Rosie!"

"*Whose* hanky?" questioned Amy.

"Nothing to do with you!" replied Rosie. She got up and went over to White Crane, stroking his head to humour him for the conversation had made him sullen. "Don't worry," she reassured the bird. "When we have Maisie back we'll take you to that magical Penglai place and get your wing fixed."

"Do I get to travel with *you*?" asked the crane, cheering up.

"Sure! Me and Andy."

Four cranes, a Red Phoenix, Blue Dragon and the colourful

Qilin flew eastwards bearing four Scots children, a Chinese postulant monk, an injured White Crane and a snake-headed black tortoise. None truly believed the curse of the Jade Snake could be overcome, but they shared a common destiny: to try!

CHAPTER 7: BATTLE OF BLUE DRAGON MOUNTAIN

"No army is invincible," Yip said quietly, looking from the dragon's cave towards the peak of the small mountain from where Blue Dragon would summon storms and rain clouds and commune with the winds to drive them across China for the farmers. Amy stood beside him in tears. He'd just told her he could never leave his mother country, although promised one day to tell her why.

"See how the hillside swarms with monkey warriors," he continued, "and so well-armed! Tomorrow, maybe running for their lives ... or not! Perhaps triumphant and all of *us* dead! Depends on destiny, Amy."

"Will the Monkey King find those things? The Red Pearl and magical staff?" she asked, wiping her tears.

Yip nodded.

"Oh yes! Blue Dragon no fool."

Blue Dragon's plan had been put into action. They'd set up camp in his cave, captured an unsuspecting monkey and, to the creature's surprise told him where the dragon's pearl and staff were hidden. The dragon had also given the captive simian detailed instruction on how to bring on the rain using these magical things (none of it true), specifying the precise time when to conjure up clouds: just before dawn! The trembling monkey had been reassured they had no intention of fighting.

"White Tiger only wants happiness for the princess," the dragon had said. "Fighting brings no happiness. And make sure the Monkey King allows no warriors anywhere near her at the top of the mountain. They could ruin the magic of the pearl and staff."

After the captive had been released, Blue Dragon explained:

"If Monkey King loves the princess he'll do everything I told that miserable monkey!"

White Tiger, Yip, Andy and Black Tortoise made war plans involving maximum use of their superior air cover. The surprise attack would be sudden and swift under cover of darkness.The princess *would* be rescued if not saved from the curse.

The following morning, before the sun came up over the mountains to the east, Yip and Black Tortoise, each effectively a mini-army, crept past sleeping monkeys in the dark forest skirting Blue Dragon Mountain. Taking up positions on either side of the mountain, below where it rose steeply to the rounded summit, they awaited the alarm that would declare battle was to commence: the cry of the Red Phoenix! Few, apart from Blue Dragon, had ever heard the unearthly sound. They hoped Monkey King would be misled into believing this had something to do with the summoning of rain.

An air attack needed to be rapid and silent. Qilin (invisible when he chose to be), bearing White Tiger, was to swoop from the south, grab the princess and vanish. White Crane and Red Phoenix would, by then, already be on their way to Penglai to warn the eight immortals that Pretty Flower was being brought by White Tiger to remove the curse of the Jade Snake. Blue Dragon would retrieve his red pearl and staff from the surprised Monkey King and, job done, all could vanish before any blood was shed ... at least human or crane blood!

Such was the plan, but White Tiger felt his mood swing wildly from excited optimism to utter despair several times a minute as he awaited the cry of the Phoenix. It was still dark, but the Qilin had insisted on invisibility. There was one problem, though. Only the Qilin would be invisible. To others, it would appear that a seated White Tiger was whizzing alone through the sky.

The minutes seemed to stretch into hours as he prayed over and again the plan would work ... and that Yip was right about the power of the healing immortal on Penglai. Would he or she rip the Jade Snake from Mei and administer some magical potion to keep the girl alive? He'd not thought beyond rescuing her from the clutches of Monkey King. Perhaps, he wondered, 'rescue' was the wrong word if she now loved the monkey. *Steal*, more like?

Whilst waiting, he checked on the others: Andy, Amy and Rosie, each astride a crane maiden. Andy was eager for battle, his re-sharpened lance at the ready with Rosie's hanky dangling from halfway up the shaft, wafting gently in a cool night breeze that blew down from Blue Dragon Mountain. Amy and Rosie had forgotten their differences. Amy said if she were to die in battle, nothing would be lost since Yip flatly refused to come back with her to Peebles.

It was like a call from another world ... a different dimension, even; the strangest sound imaginable, as if happiness and sorrow from every soul that ever lived had been turned into sound, blended somewhere deep in the centre of the earth and sent echoing through chambers of time, across the universe and back, to disturb the very air we all breathe.

On hearing the cry of the Phoenix the Qilin sped up towards the fading stars. White Tiger was aware of flashes of white beneath – three cranes – as he soared high over Blue Dragon Mountain. Sure enough they were there together on the mountain summit: Mei, in her red dress, tenderly resting her head on the Monkey King's shoulder as he held the red pearl up to a thin rim of rising sun, the golden staff in his other hand. A bubble of fury burst in White Tiger's brain. He kicked the invisible Qilin into action.

"Faster!" he urged, angrily.

The invisible creature shot earthwards. Large unseen claws reached out and snatched the girl from the monkey, lifting her into the air. The alarmed Monkey King turned and flailed the empty air with the golden staff, scanning the dark grey sky. White Tiger and the Princess were small enough also to be rendered invisible from a distance; besides, the darting zig-zag course taken by the Qilin would have made it impossible for them to be followed. Distracted, Monkey King failed to notice the approach of Blue Dragon, and as the beast's great bulk pressed down on him his only option was to give up the red pearl and golden staff to superior strength.

When Blue Dragon too was gone, the King screamed rage from the top of mountain, ordering his army to mount a full scale attack, but already the Monkey Princess, also screaming, was suspended over the China Sea on her way to the magical island of Penglai.

Or so White Tiger thought.

*****

Andy agreed that catapults, suggested by Yip, were one of the boy monk's best ideas to date. Neither Rosie nor Amy would take up any other sort of weapon. Amy said she was a pacifist like Yip (*who, Andy thought, was more 'quickiefist' than pacifist*), and Rosie also claimed to have renounced violence having spent too much time in the past with Muckle Mikey and Crazy Davie. Catapults seemed acceptable to the girls, and after a training session the night before both used these to maximum effect against the *wuya* birds. With handfuls of small stones hidden in their underwear, they took down bird after bird with amazing precision, leaving Andy, Yip and Black Tortoise free from aerial attack.

The Crane Maidens appeared immune to showers of arrows launched into the sky by monkey archers, whereas for a monkey to be hit, bullet precision, by the tip of a flying crane's beak spelt instant death. Andy, too, wreaked havoc amongst the enemy with the lance bearing Rosie's hanky, but the foot soldiers, Yip and Black Tortoise, were the real heroes.

No warrior was able to get anywhere near the postulant monk. Hurled spears were caught and returned or merely deflected. One moment he'd stand as still as a statue then two, three – perhaps a dozen – monkey soldiers would approach, and in a flash-dance of striking limbs so fast it could've been missed in a blink, the monkeys were felled. Monkeys soon ran from Yip, only to meet Black Tortoise.

The fighting power of Black Tortoise, fearsome guardian of the frozen north, was legendary across China. With an impenetrable black shell, a snake's head that saw in all directions and the speed and agility of an athlete, he sliced into a ten deep wall of armed monkeys as if cutting through butter. The remaining simian force, huge though it was, scattered in disarray down the forested mountain slopes.

The sun rose. With night and darkness left behind, forest birds sang their chorus as if nothing had happened, whilst the distant, haunting call of the cuckoo seemed to mock earthly ways.

After the battle over, Black Tortoise left the mountain and the part of China now called Shandong, heading northwards to defend his homeland against further unseen threats. Back in Blue Dragon's cave, Andy, Amy and Rosie jabbered away, reliving the triumphs of the day, laughing over the funny bits.

"Hey, Andy! The face of that monkey you called Muckle Mikey was a hoot. Took one look at you coming at him with your lance and I thought his eyes would pop out of his head. It was dead cool!"

"Yeah!" agreed Andy, beaming his pride at the girls sitting cross-legged on the ground in front of him. "Scampered up a tree like a squirrel with a firework up its bum! But you were cool too, Rosie. Amy as well. Must be loads of monkeys out there wondering why they've now got holes in their heads. Like they never even had time to see you. You two should take up archery or something back home. Might become the Scottish Borders' ladies champions!"

Amy glanced at Yip in lotus position, motionless, at the cave entrance.

"What's he *doing*?" she questioned. "I don't like it when he makes that weird noise. Scares me! Still ... he and that tortoise thing together, they kind of saved the day!"

"So did Andy!" interrupted Rosie.

"All of us did! You girls were awesome!" insisted Andy.

"Aye, but it was Yip and the tortoise guy made them all go away. Only now it's as if he's ..." Amy frowned and looked at the floor. "It's just that, well ... I could do with some practice."

"Uh?"

"Secretarial practice. With Yip. For when we get home and set up that martial arts school together."

"He's not coming, Amy! He told you. He belongs here."

"I don't believe it. He'll change his mind. He's being modest. No girl experience. That's all. I just don't like the noise he makes."

"It's called chanting," Andy said. "To tell the world he's a monk."

"He's only a postulant. Shouldn't be making funny noises like that. It's not fair!"

Blue Dragon quietly left them to bring on the rain. Long overdue, he said, what with the business of rescuing princesses ('only one,' Andy reminded him), and all that fighting eating into valuable cloud-making time. They wanted to come and watch him but, it being a dragon secret, he told them he'd have to go alone.

Clouds appeared and it began to pour. The three kids huddled together in a corner at the back of the cave. They soon ran out of battle stories. Meanwhile, Blue Dragon returned exhausted ('summoning rain clouds really takes it out of you,' he informed them), sank to the floor and fell asleep, his bone-shaking snores making slumber for anyone else out of the question. Yip, still knelt in prayer, behaved as if in a separate world and each of the other kids sat glumly thinking of his or her own life in that other dimension: modern day Peebles.

It was time to get back to the dragon noodle and go home. Their minds were already in Scotland, Amy's still stubbornly centring on where and how she and Yip could start up their martial arts school. Nevertheless, like her friends she was resigned to waiting a little longer. Returning to Peebles without White Tiger and their Chinese classmate, whose rescue had been the reason behind the whole exercise, was not an option. So they waited ... and waited ... and waited.

Hours, then days and weeks passed. Still their leader failed to return. Blue Dragon, too, began to worry about his beloved Red Phoenix. He'd never been separated from her for more than a day or two since their marriage.

Food and water were no problem, everything provided by the dragon with his magical staff and red pearl. What they lacked was information about White Tiger and the Princess.

* * * * *

"No!" objected White Tiger when the Qilin resumed his bright colours. "Stay invisible. So I can see through you and keep an eye on Mei."

The Qilin's body vanished. White Tiger flew low over the sea. Terrifying, but so much worse for poor Mei below whose feet almost skimmed the waves.

"Will it take much longer?" he asked.

No reply from the creature.

"Are we nearly there? You do know the way, don't you?"

"I think it's moved!

"What?"

"Should've reached the island ages ago."

White Tiger felt annoyed. He was supposed to be *rescuing* Mei, not torturing her.

"Can't we do something? Call out for Red Phoenix?"

"She'll be hundreds of *li* away by now."

"So where *is* this flipping island? And why are you flying so low?"

The disembodied lion face of the Qilin appeared out of thin air.

"Patience, White Tiger. We fly low in case she falls. I know she can swim. You taught her. As for the island, we keep going. Being magical it can move around."

Mei had stopped kicking. She'd gone limp. White Tiger feared for her but could do nothing. They flew on and on ... and on. Just when he decided he could take no more of not knowing what Mei was thinking, feeling or, indeed, whether she was still alive, and was planning to climb down one of the Qilin's legs to check on her, he spotted land in the far distance.

"IT'S OKAY, MEI! LAND AHEAD" he shouted down, unaware she'd not hear him with the invisible Qilin in the way.

The distant range of mountains grew from the horizon, stretching as far as he could see in both directions. Some island! So large he prayed Qilin would know where to go to find Red Phoenix, White Crane and the immortal healer, the only one who might be able to remove the accursed jade snake from poor Mei.

They landed in a field near a group of little houses close to the beach. The Qilin placed Mei softly down on the grass before touching ground himself in a series of small hops. White Tiger leapt from his back and ran to the girl. She lay on her front, face to one side, her hair an untidy tangle. He brushed the hair aside. Her eyes were closed, and for a frightening moment he feared she was dead. He felt for her pulse, as he'd done when they first emerged together from West Lake beside Hangzhou the previous year. Fast and faint, but present, thank God! He touched the Jade Snake about her neck, tempted to remove it before she awoke. Did he really believe she'd die if he were to do that?

"Don't!" warned the Qilin, watching him closely.

"What's happened to her?" White Tiger asked.

"Dunno ... but this place feels wrong. I'm sure it's not Penglai."

"Not Penglai? Well ... wherever we are I can't leave Mei lying here like this. Better carry her to those houses over there."

White Tiger tried to lift the princess on his own but it wasn't the same as when he used to carry her in the pool back home as he taught her to swim. The resourceful Qilin stretched out a broad red wing and White Tiger laid Mei's floppy body across it; a perfect stretcher on which they bore her to the nearest house with all the care befitting such a special princess. White Tiger knocked at the door. An old lady in a faded blue kimono opened it. Her eyes shone warmth and kindness as she gazed with concern at the limp body of the Chinese girl and the Jade Snake about her neck. He spoke in English but she replied in a language he'd never before heard. It certainly wasn't Mei's language. She smiled and helped him take the girl indoors, taking no notice of the Qilin who remained outside cleaning his sea-sprayed feathers.

Perhaps, thought White Tiger, *he's invisible to her?*

The woman appeared to understand Mei was in serious trouble. She and White Tiger gently placed the princess on a rolled-out mattress, draping a blanket over her body up to her chin. The woman sat beside Mei whilst White Tiger explained about Monkey King's revenge and the curse of the Jade Snake, about the battle of Blue Dragon Mountain and their frightening journey across the sea. Knowing no English, she sat and nodded, smoothing down Mei's long hair and tenderly stroking her pale cheeks.

"Can't you do anything?" begged White Tiger, desperate for Mei to open her eyes and for everything to return to normal.

The woman got up, went over to a wooden chest in the corner of the room and took out a small carved Buddha statue. She returned, lifted Mei's hand and placed the Buddha in her palm, closing the girl's lifeless fingers around it. Talking in her strange language, she took two bowls from a shelf, scooped rice and vegetables into these from a steaming pot, and gave one, with a pair of chopsticks, to White Tiger, placing the other beside Mei. She pointed to the bowl, to the Princess, and nodded.

"That's the problem! I can't wake her up!" said White Tiger.

He ate hungrily then looked greedily at Mei's untouched food, but the woman shook her head, pointed Mei, and nodded.

She spoke again, but White Tiger hadn't a clue what she was saying. She pointed to White Tiger, to another mattress in the corner, put her palms together then rested her head sideways on her hands.

She wants me to sleep. Can I trust her with Mei? Could she be in league with the Monkey King? Is this language Monkey Speak?

Half-reassured the Qilin would guard the girl he lay down on the mattress. Anyway, the language sounded nothing like monkey jabber. It was mellow and lilting. Nevertheless, he tried to remain awake behind closed eyes, just in case. He listened to the woman talking to the girl, to her movements about the room, to all other sounds until …

Another voice! He *must* have fallen asleep, for he remembered things that hadn't happened. Like Andy killing the Monkey King with his lance, Yip turning into a Buddha statue and Mei dropping into the sea and being swallowed by a whale just before he could reach her. But *this* voice was so familiar!

He opened one eye. Mei was sitting up, bowl in hand, eagerly scooping rice and vegetables into her mouth using chopsticks.

He sprang to his feet, happier than he imagined possible.

"Mei? Princess?"

He said it quietly. He certainly didn't shout. Not at Mei. Besides, he felt strangely shy, as if they'd have to become friends all over again. She looked up and into his eyes and screamed, dropping her bowl with a clatter.

CHAPTER 8: CURSE OF THE JADE SNAKE

Amy had become increasingly miserable. She didn't like the food, Blue Dragon's snoring irritated her and she could not persuade Yip to change his mind. When he wasn't lost in silent meditation, he sat and smiled and listened to her telling him about school, fashion, her parents and friends, but that made things ten times worse. It showed he cared about her, so "why waste his life in this awful place?" she whispered to Andy and Rosie.

Also, there was the Andy and Rosie thing. Andy had always fancied *her*, Amy. Everyone at school knew it. Constantly putting him in his place was part of the game. Besides, he enjoyed it. Before coming to China, Andy would've done anything to get her attention. Now she'd become a shadow and he only had eyes for Rosie. When they were back home she'd really have it out with the other girl. *She* was Andy's girl chum, after all. He'd said so himself! Now, when they slept on the cave floor with rugs Yip had found in the temple, Andy would always end up closer to Rosie in the morning. It wasn't on!

Andy and Rosie, happy with each other's company, failed to notice their friend's change in behaviour ... until the morning she went missing.

* * * * *

Mei made for the door. White Tiger tried to stop her, grabbing her red dress, but she pulled herself free and ran from the building, White Tiger in pursuit.

"AFTER HER!" he shouted to the Qilin.

The Qilin spread his wings.

"NO! WAIT!" called White Tiger fearing Mei's reaction had been caused by her awful journey held in the Qilin's claws. He sprinted after her towards the beach surprised she went so fast. Perhaps all that Tai Chi and Chinese dancing back home had kept her fit. She reached the beach and halted. A line of fishermen stood between her and the breaking waves.

White Tiger stopped. He called her name again. She turned and slowly shook her head with a look in her eyes as if staring at a ghost.

"NI ZOUKAI!" she called out.

White Tiger understood. Mei had taught him the words. Mandarin for 'go away'. She'd used them once when an over-lively dog jumped up at her as they sat together beside the river. When he edged towards her she backed away, still shaking her head. One of the fishermen came and took her gently by the arms, gesturing for White Tiger to stay still. The idea that his presence frightened her hurt him more than being been kicked in the face by a monkey, but he stepped to the side whilst the fisherman led Mei back to the house and the old woman. When he tried to follow the girl inside the woman barred his way. He watched through the open door as Mei sat down on the mattress, taking the Buddha statue again from the woman. The fisherman brought out his mattress, rolled up, and closed the door. White Tiger unrolled this beside the wall and lay down. The woman came out with a rug, more food and some water in a jug.

He remained outside all day ... and the next and the next. Soon one, two then three weeks had passed by. Several times daily, the door would open, and Mei would emerge. She'd walk down to the beach with the old woman, and White Tiger followed, hiding behind trees. She appeared strong and happy. Many times she caught sight of him and her face fell, the fear returning. The woman would shake her head and wave him away. The Qilin said little to comfort him, and seemed more distant, apparently losing interest in helping White Tiger any longer. He took to sitting in the forest away from the houses. The boy's patience was wearing thin. Did the old woman expect him to spend the rest of his life out there, alone, whilst Mei played with a toy Buddha inside?

He snapped. On sudden impulse, he burst through the door. Mei, naked in a bath tub, shrieked:

"GO AWAY, STEVIE! DON'T COME NEAR ME! I'VE NOTHING ON!"

White Tiger rushed back outside, his face as red as the girl's dress. The Qilin had gone. Something was happening and the boy didn't know what. He felt confused. Then it dawned on him. Mei had spoken in English and called him by his true name.

The old woman joined him outside. Her smile seemed to fill not just her face but the whole island. She held up one finger and nodded.

One finger? What does she mean?

* * * * *

"AMY!" Andy called from the cave entrance.

He heard only the wind in the trees and the chirping of birds. Food was missing. Yip joined him.

"Amy has much sadness in her heart," the boy monk said.

"No reason to go AWOL! Rosie! Come here. Gotta look for Amy."

"She'll be back. Having a little tantrum, I guess. She'll be a teenager soon. Teenagers are always having tantrums."

"No! Big sadness," repeated Yip. "Must find. Before the *gui* get her. Hungry Ghosts! *Gui* seek people with sadness to steal their bodies."

For Andy that was enough. Amy was still his girl chum even though he was leaning more towards Rosie. No way could he allow her to get turned into a ghost! Perhaps there'd still be monkey guerrillas in the woods. There was only one path down the mountain and she couldn't have gone far by foot. Reaching the river below, she'd surely have the sense to stay close to the water. And when they found her Andy could do a deal. Back in Peebles Amy would be his girlfriend Monday to Thursday and Rosie from Friday to Sunday ... unless, heaven forbid, the pustular monk were to change his mind!

Blue Dragon remained behind. Without Red Phoenix, he moped too much to be of use; besides, someone had to stay in case White Tiger should return with Maisie. The cranes circled above, watching out for *gui* and monkeys, whilst Rosie and the two boys, Andy with his lance, set off in search of their friend.

* * * * *

Amy began to have second thoughts when she reached the foot of Blue Dragon Mountain. What if Yip wasn't as keen on her as she was on him? She tried to dismiss the idea when she recalled the way he smiled at her. There again, he seemed to smile at everyone and everything. Why couldn't he come clean and give her a reason for not coming back to Peebles with her? No! She was right! Absence makes the heart grow fonder. She'd read that. If she were to vanish for a day or two then reappear, sad and dishevelled, he would surely fling his arms around her, sweep her off her feet and promise undying love. It was how things happened in those romance books she'd read. And if not Yip, Andy might do it and forget about Rosie.

She followed the stream a short distance then scrambled over rocks and entered the forest. She would find shelter, lie low and when the food ran out return to the dragon's cave. Should she smear mud over her face to gain sympathy before going back, she wondered? No! Yip wouldn't want to kiss her then. Maybe just tear her dress a bit more and pretend a band of monkeys had abducted her. Wow ... *that* would be romantic, she reckoned, as she looked for a cosy place to sit and have breakfast.

* * * * *

It hadn't occurred to White Tiger the Qilin might no longer feel needed. *Gone to look for food*, he thought. He'd never before considered how a creature the size of the Qilin sustained itself, even though it had originated in his mind.

When Mei came outside, refreshed after her bath and more radiant than ever, she was alone. She looked at him and no longer had fear in her eyes although clutched something in her hand as if her life depended on it. Doubtless the Buddha statue!

He followed her down to the shore where she stood in silence and gazed out to sea. She seemed to be looking for something ... or someone. The Monkey King perhaps, for she still wore the Jade Snake? She returned to the little house and the old woman. All day and all night White Tiger pondered over the change in the girl. During brief periods of sleep he no longer had nightmares. In one dream they were together in their camp beside the River Tweed, laughing over things Mei had written in her yellow notebook: secret things that caused her to blush!

That morning, on waking up, he took the notebook from his pocket and flicked through pages till he came to the one with the heart. He looked at the Chinese writing under the heart, touching the beautiful calligraphy with the tips of his fingers. He'd never thought beyond Mei's dad finishing his PhD in Edinburgh and the Wu family returning to modern Hangzhou. Could she really stay behind with his family, a bride-to-be at the age of twelve? Of course not, but the knowledge that this had been her secret wish seemed more delicious to White Tiger than summer strawberries and chocolate ice cream.

The door opened. Mei stood in the open doorway.

"She says we must go," the girl said. "Before Monkey King finds me again. Before he ..."

She paused as White Tiger scrambled to his feet.

"Princess?"

Mei raised her hand towards the boy. A shadow clouded her face.

"No! Don't ask! Not yet!"

She glanced down at the Jade Snake against her chest. The curse may have been lifted temporarily, but the snake was still there, a reminder that the Monkey King had a hold over the girl. Her other hand remained a tight fist? Had the curse been lifted only for when she held the Buddha statue?

The old woman joined them. She carried bundles of food and drink and led the children down to the beach where a dozen sturdy fishermen stood beside a boat. They bowed, as if he and Mei were royalty. One said something that sounded like *'Kon ... ee ... chee ... wa!'*

"What's happening?" White Tiger asked Mei.

"They take us in boat?"

"How d'you know? They speak a different language."

"Writing same. She write many things. I tell more when in boat but now must hurry."

"What about the Qilin? He'll return to find us gone."

Mei giggled in a way that had always filled him with happy feelings.

"Qilin a mythical creature, Stevie! Come from self. Remember?"

White Tiger shrugged his shoulders. If the Qilin came from inside him, where did the Monkey King come from? Maisie?

White Tiger helped the fishermen push the long narrow boat into the water. The sea was choppy, and one of the men lifted Mei over the breaking waves, lowering her carefully into the stern of the boat. The boy felt a stab of jealousy. For a brief, insane moment he saw the man as the Monkey King.

He splashed through the swell and heaved himself over the side of the boat, crouching beside Mei. How come girls always look good, whatever the circumstance, he wondered as water dripped from seaweed clinging to his legs?

The fishermen pushed out the boat, climbed in, and, each leaning on an oar, rowed towards the open sea. The boat sped across the water, dipping up and over waves, and the waves broke over the bow of the craft splattering the two children in the stern with silvery spray. Mei laughed again, a laugh that reminded White Tiger of the time they flew over rice fields to Blue Dragon's cave the last time he was in China. He remembered, too, the expression on her face when he'd reassured her she was alive after they'd first emerged from Hangzhou Lake at the Chinese end of the mysterious noodle of dragon sparkle.

And now? Were they still alive?

"Tell me what the old woman said to you," he asked.

"We go to Island of Penglai from Japan."

Of course! The bowing, 'Konichiwa' ... a different language but the same writing! After heading east from China without coming across the mythical island of Penglai they were bound to hit either Korea or Japan. He knew some Japanese people were also Buddhists.

"So she knows all about the island and ..." He glanced nervously at the Jade Snake. "Er ... *that* thing?"

"It's why we must hurry," the girl pointed out. "Monkey King can feel Jade Snake as well. He, too, is cursed."

"Him? How?"

Mei looked away from White Tiger. She'd turned a shade pinker.

"I remember how I felt before Buddha charm work."

She opened her small hand and showed White Tiger the Buddha statue.

"Does it ... like sort of work against the Jade Snake?"

Mei shook her head.

"I loved Monkey King. And I hated you. Like you were the very worst thing. A devil! And I hoped my husband would save me from you."

"Husband?"

"*I* thought he was. It seemed so real."

"So what happened in that little house near the beach?"

Mei laughed again.

"First I think 'Mei not monkey'! Felt funny to be monkey. Then ..."

The girl paused, her expression suddenly serious.

"Buddha like still water," she said. "In Buddha see my destiny re ... refrected ..."

White Tiger chuckled. His girlfriend still occasionally muddled up her 'l's and 'r's.

"Reflected! Your destiny?"

"Yeah! Not Monkey Princess! See only ..." She went quiet, looking down at her hands. "Can't say what see."

White Tiger felt for Mei's notebook and showed her. She gasped.

"Where you find this?" she asked.

"In the dungeon. That cage where he kept you locked up."

"Remember only beautiful palace. Big room where I dance for him."

White Tiger felt worried. Could Mei change back again? Did that little Buddha truly have the power to undo the curse? He found the page with the heart. Mei covered her mouth with her hand, her bright eyes watching him.

"You find? Must think me terrible!"

White Tiger felt bad, as though he'd been prying into her

private thoughts, but the battle wasn't over yet. He had to remind Mei who she was and who she'd *been* before the accursed Jade Snake got strung around her neck.

"So glad you no read Chinese!" she announced, her hand still covering her mouth.

Should he tell her? And was her written wish also reflected in the calm waters of the Buddha?

"The answer's 'yes'," he said, thinking about that wish, but she never heard him. The boat shot into the air, ascending the crest of an enormous wave before crashing down into the trough that followed in its wake. The children were soaked by sea deluging over the sides of the boat, and White Tiger set to baling out the water using a hollowed bamboo container.

"Could you *really* stay behind in Scotland?" he asked the girl after returning to his place in the stern.

Mei said nothing but she looked happy and he knew he'd not said the wrong thing.

The storm died down, and the fishermen made good speed. They took it in turns to rest and eat, and White Tiger and Mei also ate when hungry, drank from flasks and slept when tired. There was no further mention of the Monkey King and the boy felt no need to question whether or not the fishermen knew where they were going. It was as if the small Buddha statue Mei clutched was leading them. That little carved figure would save Mei from the curse ... and from a fate worse than death.

He hoped!

* * * * *.

"SHHH!" shushed Yip.

Andy had been explaining to Rosie how medieval knights

would joust in tournaments, how they had squires — would-be knights who sorted out their chargers ('what are they?' ... 'horses' ... 'why don't you just call them horses?' ... ''cos they charged around' ... 'Oh!'), helped them into armour and acted as go-betweens between knights and their lady-loves, delivering coded messages hidden in silk slippers or little hollow trinkets.

"You see, sometimes the lady-loves were of superior standing."

"Uh? I don't get it," puzzled Rosie. "Superior standing? Did they have to stand on boxes?"

"Boxes? No ... er ... status," corrected Andy. "Superior *status*."

Rosie's dad was a lawyer and Andy's worked in a garage. A lowly mechanic! He thought Rosie ought to know that sort of thing should not be a concern for lady-loves.

"SHHH!" repeated the boy monk.

Yip had halted at the foot of the mountain above the fast-flowing stream, alerted by a movement in the bushes out of sync with the wind song that rustled the leaves in the trees. Noiselessly, he crept on alone towards the forest. Andy envied his courage and prayed Rosie hadn't sensed the fear that had turned the back of his neck into a prickly cactus. White Tiger once told him about the *gui*, or 'hungry ghosts', and he breathed a sigh of relief when the Chinese boy returned.

"Not right!" Yip whispered. "Eyes watching all the time. Strange eyes. No talk from now on."

Not an easy one for Andy! Once, having been scolded by the teacher for talking during a boring English lesson, he muttered to Stevie sitting beside him how 'speech distinguishes Homo

sapiens from other primates and should never be discouraged!'
However, he followed Rosie in silence, his lance resting on his
shoulder, just *thinking* about girls instead of talking to one of
them. It helped to neutralize the fear. Looking at Rosie ahead,
he liked the way girls of her age changed shape, filled out a bit
and looked more important. He would hold her to that promise
to knight him with her great granddad's Japanese sword ... and
he swore he'd thump the hell out of any boy at school who
dared tease her about her red hair. She was *terrific*!

The postulant monk halted and turned.

"Down!" he whispered.

Andy and Rosie couched low beside a large rock, Rosie's
hand resting on Yip's back. Andy frowned. Not because of
where Rosie had placed her hand, but because of another rock
ahead. It moved ... on its own.

* * * * *

Twice darkness fell. Despite two more sunsets and two
risings of the sun ahead of them, nothing could discourage
those fishermen from urging the boat ever westwards. All night
they rowed. Mei kept White Tiger entertained with tales of her
childhood and travels in modern China, further ancient myths
of Chinese animals and beasts that she'd heard from her
mother's father, her *Kung-Kung*, and she also passed time by
teaching him different tones for Chinese syllables which would
completely change the meanings of words. She wrote down
things in Chinese in her book for the boy, but those last pages
that Yip had translated she avoided. The words with which she
professed her love for the monkey remained, she thought, her
secret, and White Tiger wondered why she didn't tear out the

pages and throw them into the sea? Were they also a part of the curse ... or were they now sacred to her? Jealousy played havoc with his mind.

When the oarsman up front scanning the sea suddenly stood and shouted in Japanese to the others, pointing to the horizon, it came as a relief to White Tiger. The man flapped his arms at the waves ahead. The children squinted into the sun and at first saw nothing. Then a point of white light showed. It was moving towards them. Swift and purposeful, wings outstretched.

White Tiger patted Mei's leg.

"There!" he cried. "That huge bird! I'm sure it's White Crane! Must be healed!"

"Healed?" queried Mei.

"Aye! Never got round to telling you. He got injured, poor thing. They were being chased by *wuya* birds. Andy saved his life."

"Can't be! *Wuya* birds are good!" insisted the girl.

Good? Have to watch what I say, thought White Tiger, still wary of the Jade Snake around Mei's neck.

"Sure they are," he agreed. "Just that ... well, they were pecking everyone and chasing Andy and Rosie flying on White Crane ... can't think why ... and they nearly hit this mountain, ken. Andy pushed away with his lance ... they flipped over, but White Crane hit the rock and broke his wing. Crane Maiden broke their fall."

White Tiger said no more. It seemed that to risk interfering with the Buddha's easing of the curse might destroy his chances of consolidating their fragile, renewed friendship.

White Crane circled three times before landing in the bow.

"Let *me* do the talking," Mei suggested, grinning. "Remember?"

"I remember you pinching me last year whenever you thought I upset him," the boy whispered.

Mei giggled and White Tiger felt a bit more relaxed.

"How's your wing, White Crane?" he called out. "Got your old job back, then?"

"Worse luck!" joked White Crane. "Seems they couldn't find another mug to do it, so they got me fixed!"

White Tiger had never before known the bird in such a buoyant mood.

"Red Phoenix still with you?"

"Nope! Gone back to check on Blue Dragon. Said she'd left him far too long. As soon as I could fly, she took off."

"Just the three of us again, then!"

The boy hoped the crane's presence would help remind Mei who she really was.

"We must hurry, White Tiger. I've already spotted Monkey King twice. He's desperately seeking Pretty Flower. Once we're on Penglai she'll be safe. He must know we're trying to get her there. You've still got a few hours journey left. He could easily leap out of the sky, grab the Princess and make off with her."

White Tiger wasn't sure whether Mei looked pleased or upset at the thought of this. His temper rose to the surface.

Few hours? Stupid bird! Got your wings back, haven't you?

"Why on earth don't you fly us there? Or will that be too much trouble, huh?"

White Crane sighed. Mei gave her friend a gentle pinch on the arm.

"He's no better, Princess! Didn't you teach him *anything* in Peebles? Up in the sky, exposed, Pretty Flower is a thousand times more vulnerable. With only you to protect her? Not a chance! He'd snatch her from you before you could blink an eye. Might as well take the kinder path and drown her at sea whilst she can still die. Oh, why *do* you allow White Tiger to be so silly, Princess?"

Here we go again! Couldn't those immortals have fixed that tongue of his as well?

Mei didn't reply, but White Tiger could sense her fear. *Snatched out of the sky?* He put an arm around her and she allowed him the closeness. Now he felt angry with himself for having doubted her.

"Cover her up with the rugs. Yourself, too," suggested White Crane. "Let him think these men are ordinary fishermen. He'll never imagine you'd come westwards to Penglai by sea from the Land of the Rising Sun."

"*Aren't* they ordinary fishermen?" asked the boy.

"Am *I* an ordinary crane?"

Worried any reply might be taken as offence, White Tiger said nothing. He hid Mei and himself underneath the rugs, and for the next few hours they lay side by side in the dark, moving only in response to the waves, neither daring to speak. White Crane took off to reconnoitre, returning a while later.

"I spied him!" the bird said. "We're only minutes from the beach now. I'll wait on the shore in case he sees me in the boat. Might get suspicious. I'll ... bother! He's spotted me!"

The boat rocked violently from side to side. There were screams and shouts. White Tiger put both arms around his princess and firmly held onto her ... until their cover was ripped away from them. Something yellow, brown, hideous and hairy peered down as White Tiger shielded his eyes from the bright sunlight.

CHAPTER 9: PENGLAI SHAN

A rock? Rocks don't move by themselves. Not even in this weird place!

Amy felt every bone and muscle in her body freeze. She held her breath in case whatever moved should sense the air wafting in and out through her nostrils. If only Yip or Andy were there! She'd even apologise to Andy for all her rudeness if he could appear and protect her from that thing.

The 'rock' grew slowly out of the ground, changing shape. Hard jaggy bits became smooth, and as it reached upwards the grey became pinker ... more skin-coloured. Hands budded from the body. A head with mean, hollow eyes and a mouth like a kitchen sinkhole, popped up from narrow shoulders. Long, skinny, skeleton legs pulled themselves free from the clinging soil, as if the earth was reluctant to give back its ghost to the world of the living. A bony hand stretched out towards Amy.

She tried to scream but the sound that came out was more like that of a mouse who'd just seen a cat. She threw all her food at the thing, turned and ran. She ran on to wherever she saw a gap in the dense growth of the forest, sometimes to the left, sometimes the right. She ran from every rock, fearing it, too, would turn into a 'thing' with arms and legs and hollow eyes. She heard the sound of running water. The stream! If she could reach it she'd keep running up the path, back to the cave. Yip would be there. He wouldn't let this 'thing' eat her alive.

149

She thought she was heading back towards the stream, but stopped when she realised the sound of water was behind her. Frantic, she looked in all directions, aimed for a space between two bushes and went straight through something that should have been solid.

It was a crouching figure, eating food from the ground. It looked up just before she hit it … only she hit nothing. All she felt was an icy chill. She turned, stared … and screamed. This was the very object she'd been running from … in a huge circle!

This time the scream was so loud even the *gui*, the hungry ghost, looked alarmed. It stepped backwards.

"GO AWAY!" Amy shrieked, hysterical. She picked up a stick and began hitting at the *gui*, but her stick found only cold air. The *gui*, who'd earlier been too busy scoffing food to bother too much about her, dropped a handful of rice and tilted its ghastly head to one side, taking renewed interest in the child.

'A new life in a young body?' it seemed to be thinking.

* * * * *

Andy, Yip and Rosie heard the scream. The boys took off into the wood towards the sound, shouting 'AMY! AMY!' Rosie, hampered by her long dress, tried to keep up but couldn't.

"ANDY! WAIT!" she cried out when all she could see were trees and bushes, the noise of the boys ahead having faded to silence.

Andy stopped.

What the heck would a true knight do?

He struggled briefly with the dilemma, turned and went back for Rosie. When they found Yip, he was standing between Amy and what looked like a shrinking rock, his hands together

in prayer. Amy was shaking. Rosie put her arm around the other girl and hugged her. A haunting chant, as if from another world, flowed from Yip's mouth and Andy stood and watched whilst the *gui* vanished into the ground.

Andy said nothing as they walked slowly back up the slope to the dragon's cave. Amy sobbed and Rosie held her close, whilst Yip, in the lead, head bowed, seemed lost in thought.

The appearance of a large red head over the ledge at the top of the path, in front of the cave, brought some cheer. Red Phoenix had returned. She was sure to have news of White Tiger.

* * * * *

"My Lord, my Lord!" shouted Mei, hitting out at White Tiger with her fists. "Let me go, you bully!"

White Tiger held firmly onto the girl as she fought and kicked. The fishermen beat at the Monkey King with their oars, several ending up in the water when he deflected their blows with his fearsome staff.

"Stop it! I *must* go! I'm the Monkey Princess!" Mei insisted.

A brown hairy hand lifted White Tiger up and into the air. His feet dangled over Mei. The monkey's gloating face radiated triumph, a mocking grin stretching his thick, dark lips. White Tiger's temper slammed the gong like a test-of-strength fairground hammer. He packed all his anger into a punch that hit the King full on his squishy nose. Dropping like a lump of lead when the monkey released him to rub his injured face, the boy fell on top of Mei.

"You beast!" she screamed.

She pushed him off, raising a begging arm towards the Monkey King. White Tiger grabbed the arm whilst the monkey reached down and caught hold of the girl's dress. There was a ripping sound, a flash of red and the monkey was gone. Mei as well!

* * * * *

"Sit down, girls," Red Phoenix said gently.

Using her beak, she bunched the children's rugs together into a heap and Rosie took Amy across the cave and sat with her on the soft seat thus created. Amy could not stop crying. Blue Dragon, filling the far corner of the cave with his great bulk, opened one eye, but closed it again when Red Phoenix gave him one of her 'not now, dear!' looks.

"Sorry!" exclaimed Yip.

Sorry? A great guy, thought Andy, *but completely unhinged! He saves Amy's life and says sorry!*

Yip stepped forwards and knelt on the floor before the girls. Andy feared for a moment he was going to bow down and worship them with that weird chanting of his, as if they were a couple of angels.

"Sorry," he repeated. "*So* sorry!"

Amy stopped crying.

"I ... I thought if I vanished ... just for a wee while ... you'd feel differently about me. I really meant it about you coming back to Peebles. If you care! That's why I ran away. I hoped you'd change and take more notice of me when I got back! I honestly didn't want to cause trouble."

"It's okay," said Rosie, stroking the other girl who sat sniffing back the sobs.

"No, *not* your fault," insisted Yip. "I should have explained before. Yip wish so much he could come with you to Peebles,

Amy. To start Martial Arts School. And you be my secretary." He chuckled. "Secretary wear short skirt and up-make, huh?"

Amy giggled her excitement.

"Make-up!" she corrected. "So you *will* come back with us?"

The boy monk shook his head.

"Cannot," he replied, his smile replaced by sorrow. "Must now explain why wish not come true."

Andy, eager to find out more about the mystery of the monk, sat beside Rosie. Perhaps the boy's story would also teach him more about the mystery of females. Knights needed to learn everything there is to be known about girls, and he had to admit Yip had a way with Amy. Red Phoenix and Blue Dragon also pricked up their ears.

"Once a man in our village did bad things. He was a very lazy farmer. Never work. Always fighting people."

"Sounds like Muckle Mikey!" joked Andy.

Rosie told him to shut up, so he kept his mouth firmly closed.

"Then he steal things. First food ... rice, chickens (*funny thing to want to steal*, thought Andy) ... even other men's wives (thinking of what was happening to Maisie, Andy moved up closer to Rosie). Village people turn man away. Man's wife and little son have no home. Become beggars."

By now Rosie, too, was crying. Andy wanted to hug both girls but decided it might be inappropriate. This was Yip's moment.

"Then the bad man go to temple. Steal food, steal gold and ..."

Yip went quiet, as though reluctant to take the story further.

So far, Andy failed to see what any of this had to do with him not coming back to Peebles.

"Kill chief monk."

Silence ... until Amy tearfully asked:

"That man was your father?"

Yip, staring at the ground, nodded, and Andy wondered how Amy had guessed.

"Mother cannot beg any more. Feel terrible. Think her fault. Take me to temple. Ask monks look after me. She promise her son will spend his life giving back to Buddha what her husband take away. Never see my mother again. Only five years old."

"That's no reason," sobbed Amy. "It was nothing to do with you! It's not fair!"

"Cannot break mother's promise! But ..."

Yip's smile returned.

"Would come to Peebles if father not bad man. Take different path."

"Path?" queried Amy.

"To enlightenment."

"You're not fat! Why d'you have to be made lighter?"

Yip chuckled.

"Soul, Amy! Enlightenment of soul."

* * * * *

White Tiger looked up. He saw the Monkey King dangling from the Qilin's great claws, kicking furiously as the creature sped over the waves towards the horizon. Mei wasn't with him. Not in the boat either.

A fisherman dived into the sea. White Tiger pulled himself up and gripped the edge of the tipping vessel. The fisherman swam strongly towards something red, pink and black bobbing in the water. Mei! *He'd* taught her to swim, thank goodness, but only at the swimming baths in Peebles. Her arms flailed furiously, but she stayed on the surface and soon the fisherman swam back with her to the boat. White Tiger helped to pull her over the side. Her dress was badly torn and he covered her with a rug, but she immediately tossed this aside and began hitting him again.

"Where is he? Where's my Lord? What have you done? It's all your fault!"

She pushed him away and burst into tears. That's when he saw the carved Buddha statue in the bottom of the boat. The girl must have dropped the object when the Monkey King surprised them. He retrieved it and forcefully took her hand. She struggled against him, trying to yank her arm free and even attempted to bite like a monkey would. It took two fishermen to restrain her as he slowly prized her fingers open, placed the Buddha in her palm and closed her fist, cupping his hands around it. She went quiet for a few moments.

"What ... what happened?" she asked. "W-Was I dreaming?"

"No," replied White Tiger softly. "It's the curse. You dropped the Buddha statue. I *must* get you to shore immediately. He can't reach you there."

"I'm so frightened, Stevie. I don't want to turn into a monkey!"

"You won't!"

As he put the rug across her shoulders and held her close, he prayed he was right, but on approaching the island he felt a mix of despair and hope.

The island was white. Not like snow, but a strange luminous white that shone happiness and peace: the beach, the rocks, and, beyond a forest of trees adorned with brightly-coloured flowers, steep, rugged slopes that soared upwards to the peaks of a lofty mountain ... all were white!

So this was Penglai Shan, the magical mountain island of the eight immortals! Closer to land, White Tiger saw Chinese roofs amongst the trees of the forest ... roofs of gold.

"Stevie?"

"Yeah!"

"Will I ever get rid of the Jade Snake?"

White Tiger said nothing. Only on the magical island of Penglai might he find the answer to her question.

* * * * *

"*We* could still start up a martial arts school," suggested Andy. "Like I'm sure knights were good at that kinda of stuff too. If you lose a lance or sword in battle you have to rely on martial arts. Karate means 'hands only', you know."

Amy was unimpressed.

"We'll call it the Yip Kung Fu Academy! You could still be the secretary. In a mini skirt. Good publicity!"

Amy scowled at Andy.

"No," said Yip. "Better I make Amy Temple here in China."

The girl's eyes lit up.

"An Amy Temple? What's that?"

"Near holy mountain of Emei Shan. New temple called Amy Temple, not Emei. I teach good things there. Become special for Buddha. With a room for only me to go in. To meditate on my other path."

"Other path?"

"Amy path. If mother not make that promise, Yip take Amy path. To Peebles."

"You'll think of me?" the girl asked, her eyes revealing her excitement.

Yip nodded. Amy jumped up, ran to Yip and kissed him on the lips.

"Amy, you don't do that sort of thing to monks!" Andy said.

"He's only a postulant! And I'll come back, Yip! I will! I know where the dragon noodle is. I'll come back alone when I'm old enough."

The others said nothing. They knew she'd never return, but realised the thought that one day she might do so helped her cope with feelings she did not understand.

Amy's encounter with the *gui*, and Yip's revelation, were turning points for the girl. She decided to tidy up the Blue Dragon's cave and decorate it with flowers from the forest. She scrubbed the dragon down because she thought he needed cleaning, she cooked meals and washed clothes. Andy, Yip and Rosie set about making chairs and a table from forest wood since they'd all got fed up sitting and eating on the ground.

Andy hoped the change in Amy would last at least until White Tiger returned. He wasn't too bothered when that might be, for he enjoyed making things with Rosie and spending time with her. Back home it would be different. After all, *her* father was a lawyer and *his* dad a garage mechanic. That really worried him.

"People can do without lawyers but not cars!" Rosie told him when they talked about this, but he wasn't reassured. Suppose others looked down on him? This might reflect on Rosie if she were to become his girlfriend. There was only *one* solution: he'd have to do something spectacular!

*****

A fisherman carried Mei to the beach where White Crane stood patiently waiting as White Tiger sploshed through breaking waves. Even the frothing white of the surf seemed to radiate a peculiar calmness. The fisherman bowed and said something in Japanese that sounded like '*say ...o...nara!*' The others waved from the boat. White Tiger raised his hand, hesitant, for he didn't want the fishermen to leave. He feared being alone on a magical island with a grumpy crane, whose wing had been injured, and Mei, still cursed. He knew the only thing keeping insanity away from the girl was the little Buddha statue. But when he looked at the men and their boat, and as they rode from the shore out towards the open sea and Japan, he could see these *were* no ordinary fishermen ... as the old lady who had given Mei the statue was no *ordinary* old woman.

"She's safe here but can't remain forever," said White Crane. "Quick! On my back!"

White Tiger helped the girl up then mounted behind her, one arm about her waist, his other hand firmly closed around her hand that held the Buddha.

"Like old times, White Tiger and Princess, ay?"

White Crane turned his head as he rose up into the air. There was something different about the look on the crane's face and the whiteness of his white. The grumpiness had gone and the white was like the white of the island.

159

Of course! This is where he belongs, realised White Tiger. *No wonder he felt grumpy before. And flying us to the moon last year to see Moon Rabbit? Only a magical crane could do that. A magical crane from a magical island!*

Even the air was strange. It felt like invisible silk brushing his cheeks, filling his lungs, as they glided smoothly towards the mountain. At the edge of the forest skirting the mountain was a magnificent building with roofs of gleaming gold.

"The Palace of the Eight Immortals," White Crane informed them. "It's where we're heading for. Hope *He*'s in and not out collecting her magical fruits."

"His!" corrected White Tiger.

"Her. *He*'s a she."

The boy felt uncertain. Someone at school once said there were guys around who liked to dress up as girls, and that sometimes you couldn't tell the difference. He wasn't sure he wanted to actually meet one of them.

"*He Xiangu.* A girl. Made immortal at the age of fourteen."

"Hey, cool! A teenager forever!"

"Yeah ... well the fruits she collects have healing powers. She *will* cure the princess, I know it."

Cure the princess?

The very words kicked at the burden of the Jade Snake weighing heavily on the boy's mind. Could *He* remove the snake from the girl's neck without killing her?

Closer, the palace was even more magnificent. The gold was inlaid with jewels and precious stones of every imaginable colour. Rubies, sapphires, emeralds, not to mention the amber, amethyst and jades of different shades and hues. White Tiger found out where these came from as they came in to land in the palace courtyard. From afar, the trees and bushes of the forest appeared laden with flowers, but now he saw many of the 'flowers' were jewels. Diamonds hung in sparkling clusters, branches waved budding garnets, aquamarine and turquoise whilst pearls, opals and topaz blossomed on shrubs.

The true flowers were unlike anything White Tiger had seen in Peebles or in the Botanical Gardens in Edinburgh. They were awesome, as were their scents. Some of the trees and shrubs bore bulging fruits that defied description and made the boy feel very hungry. He just hoped they'd get something to eat in the palace!

"Follow me," said White Crane.

They entered the palace by a circular moon gate of gold. Inside, the floor and high walls were the same brilliant white as the mountain. Eight scroll paintings of Chinese figures decorated one wall.

"*He!*" said White Crane, pointing with his wing at one depicting a lovely young girl in a long white robe. "I'll take you to her apartments."

The bird led the way along a bright corridor to a large hall. Mei gasped, for never before had she seen such magnificent furnishings. A large golden Jolly Buddha statue sat at the far end of the room. There were several doors leading off and White Crane disappeared through one of these, reappearing moments later with a Chinese girl even more beautiful than her painting. *Almost* as pretty as Mei, thought White Tiger, and that was saying something!

"Pretty Flower, I've waited so long to see you," the girl said.

"You too, White Tiger. At last destiny has brought you both here."

He took Mei to a long low couch of yellow and gold with blue jade dragon feet. They sat together, and the immortal held Mei's hand in hers, opening it out, lightly stroking the younger girl's fingers. She asked to see Mei's other hand still clutching the little Buddha.

"NO!" shouted White Tiger. "DON'T TAKE IT FROM HER!"

He looked up.

"What?" she asked.

"The Buddha the old lady gave her! Without it the curse'll come back. Please don't do it!"

Mei opened her hand to show *He* the little Buddha statue.

"My mother did well," *He* said. "But *here* the princess remains healed. Don't worry! The Jade Snake can't touch her."

"Your mother? Japanese?" queried White Tiger.

He chuckled.

"Oh, she gets around!" she replied. "You know, it wasn't the Buddha who really saved your friend. Remember what Moon Rabbit told you? About Yin and Yang?"

White Tiger remembered thinking they were a couple of circus clowns.

"The *qi* force is so strong between Pretty Flower and White Tiger the curse of the Jade Snake could never be complete. I have no healing to do."

White Tiger looked on anxiously as *He* took the Buddha from Mei's hand.

"See!" she exclaimed.

Mei looked at White Tiger with sadness but there was no longer hatred in her eyes. The sadness was because of the times they'd had together in the past beside the River Tweed, and memories of her home and her parents in Peebles.

"But what about the Jade Snake? Can't you just take it off her? Chuck it away?"

"If only it were that simple!"

"You mean ...?"

White Tiger began to feel cross. They'd come all this way to some weird island to be told the Jade Snake might never be removed! Sure, he could ask that they spend eternity together in this palace of gold, breathing the strange air, smelling those delicious smells, but it wasn't what Mei wanted. He knew from her expression.

"Look, White Crane said you'd fix things! He risked his life ..." White Tiger began, his anger frothing.

Mei was looking at him, shaking her head. It was as good as her giving him a little pinch and he shut up.

"Your destinies lie beyond here in another world," continued *He*. "But only magic can allow anyone other than the Monkey King to remove the Jade Snake from the princess. I may be immortal but I'm no magician."

"So? We ask Monkey King very politely to remove the snake if Mei apologises for doing nothing wrong last year?"

He smiled.

"Maybe that might've worked if she wasn't also a part of the monkey's destiny."

White Tiger didn't want his girlfriend to a part of Monkey King's anything, least of all his destiny.

"What d'you mean?" he asked.

"The Monkey King changed. Because of her. Her dancing, her beauty ... the fact she's so special. His anger turned to love. Didn't you ever wonder why *all* the children at school like her?"

Yeah, the boy thought. *Even Crazy Davie asked her out, the creep!*

"There are only two paths the Princess can follow when she leaves Penglai. Become a Monkey Queen for all eternity, and dance for her lord, or return to Peebles without the Jade Snake. If she chooses the second path, she must take the risk."

Risk? This wasn't going the way White Tiger expected.

"There's a magician called Anqi Sheng. Mostly, he's invisible. You must call for him from the top of Penglai Shan. If he thinks his magic has the power to remove the Jade Snake then perhaps he'll appear. But nothing's certain along the Princess's second path."

"If not?"

"The second path'll lead to the death of Pretty Flower."

White Tiger glanced nervously at Mei. It wasn't his decision. Certain immortality as the Monkey Queen or an uncertain future along the second path? The girl was staring at the Buddha statue now in *He*'s hand. White Tiger remained silent. He'd forgive her if she were to choose the first path. After all, who wouldn't?

"We go together," Mei said without further hesitation. "Second path!"

"First some food and drink!" insisted *He*.

She clapped her hands, a servant appeared as if from nowhere and soon returned with bowls filled with rice and cups of a delicious, sweet-tasting drink. However much they ate and drank, the bowls and cups remained full.

"Here on Penglai we never run out of food and drink!" chuckled *He* on seeing White Tiger scratch his head as he wondered why he couldn't seem to empty his rice bowl.

White Tiger and Mei were taken to the bottom of a trail zig-zagging up to the gleaming summit of Penglai Shan. White Crane told them *he* couldn't take them and that they'd have to go alone. The top of the mountain was from where he'd once emerged when the first of the immortals arrived at Penglai and needed a crane for transport. If he were to return to the summit he might vanish back into the mountain. The immortal *He* could have gone with them but was way behind schedule with all the other things she had to do.

They set off, and Mei must have read White Tiger's mind for she took hold of his hand.

"Please don't worry," she tried to reassure him. "We're together again. This makes Mei happy. Whatever happens I'll *never* take the first path!" When she flashed her usual smile at him the dark thoughts clouding the boy's mind vanished.

"Race you to the top then!" he said.

They ran and scrambled up the slope towards the blue of the sky, panting and giggling.The magical air of Penglai revived their energy with every breath and near the top they ran even faster. Triumphant, they held hands again as they stood on the summit looking out across the white, green and gold of the island. Apart from a few small puffy white clouds, the sky was blue; bluer than White Tiger had ever before seen. In the distance, across the sea, were the other three islands of Penglai.

Beyond, resting on the horizon, White Tiger could just make out Mainland China.

They seemed so wonderfully alone but White Tiger's happiness faded as he began to have doubts. It must have shown on his face for Mei gave him a gentle pinch on the arm as in the old days. She was still grinning.

"No feel sad! Please!" she insisted. "We call for magician now. Together!"

"Okay. Count of three ..." agreed White Tiger.

"ONE ... TWO ... THREE ... ANQI SHENG!" they shouted into the cool breeze.

Nothing! They tried again. Silence! White Tiger saw a tear appear in the corner of Mei's eye.

"Third time lucky, as we say in Peebles," he said, brushing away her tear with the back of his hand.

"ANQI SHENG!" they yelled. The boy thought his lungs would burst.

One of the puffy clouds began to move towards them. White Tiger noticed it was different from the others. Brighter, its whiteness was like the whiteness of the mountain. He squeezed Mei's hand. The cloud drifted to within feet of the children then halted. Something translucent, perched on the cloud, gradually took form. The outline of a seated figure showed, and feature by feature this turned into an old man with a beard, exactly like the old man he and Rosie had spoken to in the Chinese restaurant in Peebles only dressed in a long white robe.

"You?" queried White Tiger.

Mei glanced at the boy, her eyes wide.

"You know him? Anqi Sheng?"

Suddenly it made sense to White Tiger. The magician had been with them all along. He nodded.

"Princess Hua-Mei, are you ready?" the magician asked in a voice that blended with the wind. Mei looked anxiously at her boyfriend.

"Hold me please," she asked and White Tiger put his arm around her.

Anqi Sheng drifted towards them, reaching out with his hand. He lightly touched the Jade Snake before lifting it away from the girl's chest. He spoke softly in Chinese and the boy prayed the words would work their magic. Mei closed her eyes as he raised the snake up over her head. Tears streamed down her cheeks and White Tiger held his breath.

The girl was still standing when Anqi Sheng drifted backwards, the Jade Snake dangling from his hand.

"WAIT!" White Tiger called out.

Anqi Sheng hovered.

"So ... *you* must be the Jade Emperor's messenger!" White Tiger said. "It was *you* left that message for Mei and me last year, right? You've controlled the end of the dragon noodle in the River Tweed ever since the Romans were in Scotland."

The ancient magician winked at the boy.

"Like I've been telling everyone, White Tiger is very wise ... very clever!"

"And those ducks by the river where Mei fell in last year? Were they yours as well?"

Anqi Sheng chuckled.

"Oh yes! The ducks! I enjoyed creating *them*!"

A thought occurred to White Tiger. He frowned.

"But the Monkey King left a letter too. Was that also you?"

"Monkey King considers his destiny to one day become Emperor of Heaven ... in place of the Jade Emperor. He now believes having a human queen will help that destiny come true."

Could the magician be a double agent, also working for the monkey?

Anqi Sheng saw into the boy's mind:

"Monkey King already has his own messengers. And with the Princess he might succeed in becoming immortal if he loves her."

"He doesn't! He wants to use her. That's all."

White Tiger, angered, glanced at Mei, but her expression gave nothing away.

"I have a question," the girl said.

"Yes, my child."

"Will you ask Jade Emperor please to turn Lady Silkworm back into a beautiful young girl? Not fair that she still hangs on a tree because she didn't want to marry a horse!"

"She made a promise she couldn't keep."

"Still not fair!"

"So you are a part of *her* destiny as well as White Tiger's and Monkey King's, Pretty Flower."

"And Crane Maiden?" added White Tiger "Why can't she stay a maiden forever and return to her husband and son?" Anqi Sheng merely nodded thoughtfully. "I've another one, too," the boy continued. "If we do get home to Peebles and Mei has to go back to modern China after next year, will the Monkey King be able to get to her? Are there dragon noodles that travel only through time here in China?"

"These are questions for which even the Jade Emperor has no answers. Now hurry! Monkey King really loves the princess in his own way. He'll do anything to keep her in China. Return to the dragon noodle now! Before he stops her from reaching it. Go directly!"

"To Hangzhou West Lake? But the others? Andy, Rosie and Amy? And the boy monk, Yip? They're waiting for us in the dragon's cave in Shandong. We can't just leave them there!"

"Go immediately! No time to waste!"

"But ...?"

The old sage was becoming indistinct, his white robe turning blue against the blue sky. He was disappearing.

"At once!" he insisted before man and cloud vanished.

The words merged with the breeze and were followed by a hollow silence which White Tiger felt should be filled with all the music ever invented. He felt so happy! Mei was alive, the Jade Snake gone! They'd go to the dragon noodle and return directly to Peebles. Things would return to normal. He had every confidence Andy could look after himself and the girls. He was a great legionary. Besides, one of the immortals might get word to him ... or the magician, perhaps?

But there *was* no music.

"Thanks," he whispered to the emptiness.

"*Xiexie*, Anqi Sheng!" added Mei.

They ran down the mountainside, agile as mountain goats. White Crane was waiting and seemed rather alarmed when they jumped onto his back and told him to make haste to Hangzhou.

"Bother!" he exclaimed. "Why not the Blue Dragon's place at

Tai Shan? I'd rather hoped I could take Rosie. Together with the Princess, of course."

White Tiger winked at Mei.

"Oh, give White Crane a little pinch, Princess! He's got a thing about Rosie. Thinks she's gorgeous."

The girl laughed.

"Aren't many people in China with red hair like Rosie!" she said.

They soared up and over the golden palace and the forest of jewel trees, gliding down to fly low over the sea at a speed that reduced the waves to a blur. Staying just above the waves, explained the crane, made it less likely the Monkey King would spot them from on high as he leapt from island to island looking for Mei.

Sort of like dodging radar? thought White Tiger.

On sighting land, the crane turned southwards, following the coast-line towards Hangzhou ... and uncertainty.

The joy White Tiger had felt on Penglai Shan after the Jade Snake had been removed from Mei was soon replaced by fear. The long rip in the girl's dress was proof of the monkey's determination to have the princess for himself. The curse had been lifted but the cause, the Monkey King's revenge and his wish to displace the Jade Emperor, remained an ever present threat.

CHAPTER 10: SOMETHING SPECTACULAR

The following morning Andy was up late. He'd been vaguely awake earlier after hearing noises of people moving about (*Yip saying his prayers?*) but had decided knights need extra sleep so he'd kept his eyes closed and had drifted off again.

"Where's Amy?" he asked, looking around. "And Yip?"

The cave echoed with the deep snores of the dragon, a huge, blue hump at the back of the cave with Red Phoenix a snoozing, feathered red bump beside him.

"Went out," replied Rosie, busily preparing breakfast for the two of them. "With Yip. To the temple. Said she wants to find out more about temples if there's gonna be an Amy Temple on Emei Shan."

"Oh! Well, as long as they don't encourage the hungry ghosts!"

"They won't! Took one of the crane maidens. Should be back any moment. Dumplings?"

"Uh?" queried Andy, stretching and yawning.

"D'you want dumplings for breakfast?"

"Again? Oh ... aye! Sure!"

He was fed up with dumplings but didn't want to offend Rosie by saying so. Not when he was trying to impress the girl with something spectacular. Squatting beside her, he stabbed at a dumpling with a chopstick. He hadn't mastered chopstick technique like Stevie, but then Stevie had a Chinese girlfriend. Eating with chopsticks was an essential part of the boy's lifestyle. As for himself, doing things that might make a lawyer's daughter look up to him was far more important.

His head was beginning to fill with thoughts of all the spectacular things he could try out when noises outside diverted his attention: bird talk mingled with Amy's shrill, excited voice and Yip's deeper, calming voice. Amy, breathless, dashed into the cave.

"Not more ghosts, Amy, please!" pleaded Andy before shoving another dumpling into his mouth.

"No!" exclaimed the girl. "Much worse than that! We must leave at once. Wake up Blue Dragon and Red Phoenix. The cranes are waiting for you."

"Amy, are you mad? What about Stevie? And Maisie?"

"No time, no time! Hurry!"

Assuming they were about to be attacked, Andy stuffed a couple more dumplings into his pocket and picked up his lance.

"Rosie! Remember, stay close!"

He turned to look at the blue and red sleeping creatures at the back of the cave.

"Hey, Blue Dragon ... wake up, dude!"

The dragon snorted, opened an eye then closed it again.

"So ... which direction are they attacking from?" Andy asked Yip who sat astride one of the cranes at the cave entrance.

"Attacking? No attacking!"

"Well ... what's the fuss about? Amy interrupted us! Rosie and I were having quality time together, weren't we?"

"Amy's right. Must leave now!" insisted Yip.

"Without White Tiger? Hang on! He's my best mate. Can't just abandon him, can we, Rosie?"

"At the temple ..." began Yip, trying to explain. "Something ..."

"It was so cool," Amy butted in. "Like Yip was bowing before the golden statue ... teaching me how to do that Buddhist stuff ... and it came to life!"

"Huh! Go on at me for believing in King Arthur and now you're saying the statue came to life? Sure you've not been eating magic mushrooms?"

"Honest! It spoke to Yip. I stayed down. Too scared to look ... well ... peeked a teeny bit but that's not really looking ... and ... um, where was I?"

"Lord Buddha say Jade Snake curse is broken," explained Yip. "Princess free but more danger now for all of us. Monkey King try anything to keep her in China."

"You mean ... he might sort of stop us reaching the dragon noodle? Block it off or something?"

"Not might ... *will*! Must go immediately. Quick!"

"But ... what about *them*?" Andy jerked a thumb at the Blue Dragon and Red Phoenix.

Yip shrugged his shoulders.

"Can't say. If in right mood might help. Come!"

Andy helped Rosie onto the back of Crane Maiden and climbed up behind her, clutching his lance, whilst Amy mounted the third crane sister. The three birds leapt into the air and sped forwards like ancient, oriental hover jets sweeping down from the mountains, over fields of corn and rice, little villages and snaking rivers. Andy felt as if he'd been transported into the fast forward of a DVD movie. Soon, he saw other mountains, some dotted with temples, a sprawling town, and beside this, a large lake: Hangzhou West Lake where it all began.

The boy now feared the worst. The lakeside was crawling with monkeys and the roofs of the town were black. Closer, he saw they were covered with *wuya* birds. Even from on high the noise of screeching birds and jabbering monkeys was deafening. Little wonder the streets of Hangzhou were empty for who would dare to venture out? Yip's crane banked and glided down towards a temple near the shore-line, the only building without birds on its roof. Andy's and the other cranes followed.

Whilst they were passing over the temple, a swarm of monkeys emerged from the entrance carrying a vast golden Buddha statue, on its side, towards the lake. Not a *Jolly* Buddha. The figure was fully clothed, with no belly button showing and in a pose of serene meditation. Beyond, at the edge of the water, something was happening.

"DOWN THERE!" Andy shouted to Crane Maiden who flew in an arc round the temple. The others had already landed at the back of the building, but, carefully aiming his lance, Andy had his own plan.

"Go, bird, go!" he urged digging his heels into Crane Maiden as if she was a medieval knight's charger.

"Andy ... what are you doing? I'm scared," said Rosie.

"Look! By the water! Stevie and Maisie!"

Surrounded by a circle of jeering monkeys, White Tiger and Mei stood knee deep in the water. The boy held onto one of

Mei's arms and a monkey in fine gold and yellow garments, wearing a crown, was pulling at the other arm. The girl was screaming.

"Close your eyes, Rosie! Here we go ... YARRAHOOO!"

Crane Maiden shot from the sky like an arrow. The tip of Andy's lance hit Monkey King square on the nose. He released his hold on Mei and tumbled backwards into the water. The monkey warriors paused. The crane skimmed the water before circling and joining her sisters behind the temple. Andy jumped down to help Yip, already in engaged in battle with the simians.

"PROTECT THE GIRLS!" he yelled to the cranes.

Amy and Rosie had come under attack from squadrons of *wuya* birds, and were beating at them with their hands. The three cranes flew to the girls and, wings outstretched, covered them like the shell of a large white feathered tortoise. They used their long necks and pointy beaks with fearsome effect against their avian cousins. From under cover of the cranes, the girls scooped up handfuls of small stones and, using their catapults, fired these randomly into the monkey horde.

All fought bravely, but were hopelessly outnumbered. Andy knew they would die.

Or *would* they? Yip was amazing. Flailing a couple of monkey swords like propellors, he cut a path through the enemy line round to the front of the temple. Andy and the girls followed in his wake. The monkeys carrying the Buddha statue had reached the water and were busy tilting it upright.

"*Must* stop them!" called Yip. "They try to cover Dragon noodle with Buddha. If gold of statue merge with edge of noodle, magic can seal forever. Cannot escape and Monkey King will get his prize. Princess Hua-Mei!"

Andy looked up.

"Not so easily, dude!" he said.

The sky was filled with blue and red. Blue Dragon and Red Phoenix had appeared from nowhere. The monkey soldiers scattered as Red Phoenix swept over the town, and the terrified *wuya* birds flew from the roofs in a swarm heading out over the lake. She then turned her attention to fleeing monkeys, grabbing some in her talons, flinging them aside whilst stabbing others with her powerful beak. The birds now gone, people streamed from the town, armed with whatever weapons they could find, to help the children. But it was what was happening at the edge of the lake that caught Andy's attention. For a few moments he paused and stared as the monkeys fled.

The Monkey King, his eyes ablaze with fury, held a wicked-looking staff. He was advancing towards White Tiger who, unarmed, now stood in front of Mei. Andy had noticed something glinting in the dragon's mouth. The beast flew over his friend and dropped whatever it was into the boy's hands. Monkey King halted his advance, for White Tiger now also held a staff, and no ordinary one! He waved the Blue Dragon's magical golden staff at his foe. Monkey King was only too aware of its powers, for he'd stolen it himself the previous year. Before becoming bewitched by the beauty of the Princess and her dancing, this whole exercise had been about exacting his revenge on the girl for stealing back the golden staff and red pearl.

Their roles reversed, White Tiger was now on the attack, though still shielding Mei as he edged towards the monkey and the Buddha statue. Andy knew they only had a few moments respite for the retreating monkey warriors had halted and were regrouping.

"To the statue, girls! Quick! Before they seal off the dragon noodle! Hold the monkeys back, Yip!"

"But ...?" began Amy, glancing lovingly at the boy monk as he bravely fought off a renewed attack from the simians.

"NO BUTS, AMY! RUN!"

Monkey King had been re-joined by several of his troops. Whilst some of them battled against White Tiger with slashing swords, the King and several monkeys struggled to lift the heavy statue into position over an intense beam of light that identified the spot where the dragon noodle entered this alien world of the past. The light was fading as Andy splashed into the water and dived under the surface, holding his lance like a harpoon in front of him. He stabbed at the legs of Monkey King and his accomplices, forcing them back. Aware of White Tiger above, fighting with a fury that would have impressed the most fearless of Roman legionaries (*and* King Arthur!) he jammed the lance under the edge of the statue, lifting it enough for slim young bodies to slide underneath and into the noodle. He wedged a rock into the space, surfaced, gasped for air and cried out:

"Under the statue! Quick. Maisie first, Rosie next, then Stevie with Amy. I'll follow in the rear!"

At last a true legionary ... or knight ... or whatever!

Mei seemed reluctant to leave the protection of White Tiger. Andy grabbed the Chinese girl and pulled her to the statue. Rosie got her to breathe in and out deeply before Andy pushed them both below the surface and through the gap beneath the Buddha statue.

"Stevie, bring Amy! She can't swim!"

White Tiger sent Monkey King flying with a humungous wallop across the chest, threw the golden staff as far as possible, praying Blue Dragon would get it before Monkey King, and disappeared, holding Amy, into the brightness of the dragon noodle. Monkey King dithered, unable to decide whether to go for the golden staff or the dragon noodle. That moment of indecision cost him both. As Andy squeezed under the edge of the statue, pushing away the rock and snapping off the end of his lance, Blue Dragon swooped down and picked up his golden staff. The Buddha statue slammed down above Andy and the boy felt himself sucked backwards into the blinding noodle of dragon sparkle, twisting and turning. Somersaulting to face the right way, he saw White Tiger and Amy ahead as they swirled and twirled in the dragon sparkle until his head burst above the water surface ... in the River Tweed at Peebles.

* * * * *

A strange white cloud hovered above the lake beside the ancient city of Hangzhou. Those involved in the battle raging on the shore of the lake would not have noticed the gradual appearance of a bearded old man dressed in white, sitting on the cloud. He sat motionless, apart from raising one hand above a partly submerged golden statue of the Buddha. In a flash, the statue, cloud and seated figure were gone; no longer did that eerie circle of brightness illuminate a small patch of water on the lake.

When the battle was over, a large white crane flew from Hangzhou high over the China Sea to the magical mountain island of Penglai, a place that only two mortals have ever visited.

The Blue Dragon and Red Phoenix returned to a cave near the holy mountain of Tai Shan in a province now known as Shandong. Three cranes went back to a magical lake that transformed them into beautiful young women, one to be reunited with her husband and son, whilst in the far west of China a girl, once changed into a giant silkworm for refusing to marry a horse, became a lovely young woman again.

A young postulant monk journeyed alone across China with sadness in his heart to build a new temple on another of the five holy mountains, Emei Shan.

CHAPTER 11: YIN AND YANG

"Cool, Andy! You saved my life! And ..." Maisie paused.

Destroyed her chance of becoming immortal?

Stevie glanced anxiously at Maisie. Unlike the other four, she still wore Chinese clothes. The rip down the front of the girl's red dress, from when Monkey King made a grab for her, was the only surviving evidence of what had happened. Although they'd been in China for weeks, they had no idea what day it was back in Peebles.

"Andy's a big hero, now! Like White Tiger!" the Chinese girl said, grinning.

Stevie felt better.

"Oh Andy, what you did was *so* spectacular!" added Rosie.

Spectacular? At last!

"Aye ... well, good word that! I like it!" Andy said, playing bashful. He wondered whether medieval knights felt the same way when bowing to their lady loves after being victorious in a joust. But what would the girl tell her lawyer father?

Amy stood apart, her eyes wet with river water mixed with tears.

"What's up, Amy?" asked Stevie, looking from her to Rosie and Andy. He was getting the message that Rosie and his co-legionary were pretty comfortable with one another although he knew all about Andy's 'undying love' (his friend's exact words) for Amy. Had the other boy's passion finally died in

China? Would he now be spared all those earfuls about Amy from Andy?

"It's Yip," explained Andy. "She's fallen in love with him and he couldn't leave China. He's a monk, you see."

"His kung fu was awesome!" said Stevie. "Never seen anything like it. Better than Bruce Lee any day!"

"Aye ... that's Yip! But he stayed behind to build an Amy temple on a holy mountain ... so you shouldn't feel too bad, Amy. And you're still my girl chum. Stevie's as well ... right, Stevie?"

"Come on you lot! Better hit the Police station!"

"Stevie ... take me home first. Please!"

"Of course, Maisie. I'm so sorry! Just wanna do this right. I ..."

Maisie smiled and gave the boy a gentle pinch on the arm.

"Everything you do is right," she said.

In the High Street they stopped off at a clothes shop.

"You're the missing Chinese girl!" a surprised shop assistant said to Maisie. "Thank God you're alive! Do the police know?"

"Oh, the police know everything already. I told them before we rescued her," replied Stevie.

"So brave!" Maisie added.

"And the Monkey King ripped this dance dress of hers, you see, so I wondered whether ..."

"Monkey King?"

The lady shop assistant tried, unsuccessfully, to hide a grin.

"The police looked like that too! Anyway, have you got something she could change into? My parents'll pay you back," Stevie promised.

"Oh, forget the money! Come here, sweetheart! Let's get you out of that tattered, wet dress."

Maisie emerged from the dressing room in jeans and a tee shirt. She'd left the torn red dress on the floor and Stevie could tell she was reluctant to touch it again.

"It reminds her of Monkey King," he told the woman. "Could *you* give it to the police? They should check for monkey DNA or something. I'd better take Maisie home now."

"And the other girl?" the shop assistant asked, looking at Amy standing alone and sobbing.

"She'll get over it," Andy explained. "Her boyfriend's a monk and got left behind in ancient China."

"Oh, he did, did he?"

"Mmmm! But it's okay, 'cos he's naming a temple after her on one of the five holy mountains."

But the woman was no longer listening. She dialled the police before the children left the shop and an officer was waiting for Stevie and his victorious army at the Wus' house. As Mrs Wu, then Mr Wu, hugged their daughter, Stevie, Andy, Rosie and Amy all spoke at once:

"We'd none of us be here if it hadn't been for Yip!" Amy insisted, still sobbing her heart out. "He's just so nice!"

"Uhuh!" The police officer's jaw dropped.

"Like I kept trying to tell you lot, it *was* the Monkey King!" insisted Stevie."He kidnapped Maisie out of revenge for getting back Blue Dragon's magical staff and red pearl ... but didn't reckon on all her friends turning up in China! But I guess Blue Dragon *really* saved us. By giving me the staff. And ..."

The police officer nodded.

"No!" exclaimed Rosie. "What about Andy? He was awesome! Remember how he toppled Monkey King with his lance when we flew at the creature on the back of that crane. And *he* was the one who helped us escape. By lifting up the Buddha statue. That was brilliant!"

"Mmmm!" agreed the police officer.

"That was for *you*, Rosie," explained Andy. "I wanted to do something spectacular just for you!"

"Oh Andy, you're so sweet!"

"Ahem!"

The police officer cleared his throat with embarrassment.

"We have this red dress from the clothes shop, you see. Maisie's, they tell us. It's been ripped, and ..."

He removed the garment from a clear polythene bag and held it up for all to see.

"NO!" screamed Maisie, hiding her face against her father's chest. "Don't make me see it again! Please, *Baba*!"

Mr Wu stroked his daughter's long hair.

"Mei, tell the policeman the truth. Who gave you that dress? Was it Stevie? And did *he* rip it? I won't be angry with you."

His eyes spelt danger as Stevie glanced at him. He'd never before seen Mr Wu look at him like that. The man was a land-mine about to explode.

"White Tiger ... Stevie ... he say the truth, *Baba*! Dress from Monkey King. Angry with Mei for getting Blue Dragon's things back last year. Wanted to teach me lesson. Then he changed. When I dance for him in ... in that dress ... he always stare at me and ..."

Maisie paused and looked across at White Tiger as if unsure how much to say.

"He wanted me to become Monkey Queen and be immortal. He put Jade Snake round my neck and ..."

Stevie recalled that awful period when the girl no longer seemed to see him as he was, when they'd been prized apart by a magic that he feared might never be undone.

"But White Tiger rescued me! Like Moon Rabbit say, *Baba. Yin* and *Yang!*"

"Please," Mr Wu said to the police officer. "My daughter's not well. The other children must go home. And Mei, whatever happened we must get to the truth!"

He glowered at Stevie. It was clear he regarded Stevie as ring-leader of his daughter's staged kidnapping, perhaps only returning her because he'd got cold feet.

"We won't press charges for wasting police time," the officer told Stevie and his parents, "but any more nonsense, and ... well, I'm warning you!"

Stevie blew his top:

"That red dress! It's our evidence. Aren't you gonna do anything about it? Check for monkey DNA or something!"

But the officer merely repeated his warning and left.

The following day at school, Andy asked Rosie whether she'd told her dad about the spectacular things he'd done.

"Nope! He gave me a hell of a row, though. I think he got an earful from the police same as Stevie's parents."

"But he's gotta know!" Andy insisted.

"What?"

"About what I did with my lance. Because he's a lawyer!"

"But ..." Rosie looked puzzled. "What's *that* got to do with anything?" she asked.

"Well, being a lawyer he might ... um ..."

Andy suddenly felt awkward. For once in his life he seemed lost for words.

"Yes?"

"Will you be my girlfriend?" the boy asked at last.

Rosie checked to see no one was watching and gave him a hurried kiss on the cheek.

"Of course! Why?"

"I ... er ... I thought a lawyer might only accept someone like me as his daughter's boyfriend if I did something spectacular. My dad's only a garage mechanic, ken."

Rosie stared at the boy.

"Who cares? You're not *Dad's* boyfriend!" she pointed out. "D'you think that matters to me, anyway?" The girl grinned. "I do know what he'd say if I told him, though. 'The world can do without lawyers but not garage mechanics. Everyone would be stuck at home, wouldn't they, without cars?' Dad's got a pretty low opinion of lawyers, you know!"

"What? I don't believe you!"

Rosie gave him a jokey punch in side as they enjoyed a good laugh together. But Stevie and Maisie, sitting side by side over lunch, were not laughing.

"Your father *can't* forbid you from seeing me! Never! I won't allow it!"

Stevie was devastated to hear what Maisie said that morning, and his temper now boiled to the surface.

"Mustn't go against *Baba*," she insisted. "So sorry!"

She began to cry. He so wanted to put his arm around her, only couldn't. Not at school. He'd get reported and Mr Wu would be even more determined to separate them.

"I'll fix it! Prove I wasn't lying. Wait here!"

Stevie found Andy and Rosie and explained his plan. After school, Ross would drive the boys to police headquarters in Hawick and they'd insist on seeing the Chief Superintendent. He'd demand they analyse Maisie's red dress. Radio-carbon and DNA testing! If they refused he'd speak to his MP and MSP and tell the newspapers and TV news channels that the police had botched up the case.

That evening he saw the Chief Superintendent and made an offer the police could not refuse. He'd stay silent only if they did the tests and told Mr Wu what they were doing and why.

The following day, Maisie, smiling, told Stevie her *baba* thought he'd been too harsh and perhaps they might be allowed to meet up occasionally under supervision. A month later the forensic results on the dress came through. Stevie's and Maisie's parents were called to the police headquarters, and Stevie, alone at home, could barely stay still. He went from room to room, picking things up for no reason, his mind elsewhere, fearing the result of the investigation might end his relationship with Maisie forever. He ran to the door when he heard his dad's car pull up outside.

"I told them my son never lies!" his dad said.

"What, Dad? What did they say?"

But the phone rang before Mr Scott could answer. Stevie picked it up. Maisie was at the other end of the line, sobbing so much he had difficulty making out what she was saying. Only the word 'happy' was intelligible.

"You're happy, Maisie? I don't understand. What are you crying for?"

"No go back to China! *Baba* say must stay here. In Scotland."

"What ... I mean ... Maisie ...?"

Stevie wiped the back of his hand across his eyes. No legionary should be seen wet-eyed!

"Red dress a thousand years old," the girl said at last. "And find monkey DNA on it! White Tiger so clever, like Mei tell Blue Dragon! Father say not safe go back to China. Apply for more job here till ..."

"Till?"

Maisie went quiet, as if she were about to say something she shouldn't.

"Your yellow notebook?"

Maisie giggled.

"Yip told you what I wrote? Underneath the heart?"

"Aye ... well, suits *me* just fine!"

That weekend Mr Wu threw a party for all five children. There was enough food for a whole troop of Chinese legionaries. Maisie wore a yellow Chinese dress. Andy had on a kilt and dress shirt because, as he put it to Rosie, both lawyers *and* mechanics can wear that sort of stuff in Scotland. Rosie wore pink because Andy had said he liked her in pink, whilst Amy wondered about wearing Buddhist orange and brown, but turned up, instead, in a bright blue mini-skirt and a skimpy top that revealed her belly-button. Suitable for a secretary, she told the boys. She was still determined to open a

Kung Fu school in Peebles and call it the Yip School of Martial Arts.

"Great idea, Amy," Andy said, "but who's gonna do the teaching?

Amy shrugged her shoulders.

"I'll find someone. At school, maybe?"

Andy thought this highly likely if she went around in clothes like that.

The real reason behind the party was to allow Mr Wu to get reassurance from all the children that what had happened to them would remain forever a secret. The police had closed the book on the case and the red dress that Maisie feared so much had been destroyed.

Maisie spelt out one condition for her and Stevie's continuing friendship: that he would *never* mention the word monkey, *never* make her see any movies, or have any books with monkeys in them and she absolutely refused to go to a zoo ever again … anywhere in the world!

So, for Stevie and Maisie, monkeys ceased to exist.

EPILOGUE: PATHS OF THE MONKEY KING

"It's your fault! You never gave me chance! With the Jade Emperor on White Tiger's side I was outnumbered. I loved the Princess! She would have been so very happy as the immortal Monkey Queen!"

Monkey King, standing in the Buddha's huge hand, angrily shook his fist at the great face beaming benignly down at him.

"Oh Monkey King, why do you always wish to blame your Lord? I make no choices, no decisions and have no influence over the Jade Emperor. I only point the way, but you always choose the other path."

"Lord Buddha, you made me a promise. Immortality if I proved my love for the Princess."

"Yes," replied the Buddha, "but that wasn't the path you followed. If you want to find the right path learn from your mistakes. Take the same path and you'll end up again in my hand, blaming me."

"How come White Tiger got the Princess?"

"He didn't. He merely allowed the Qi force to flow between them. He had a temper. The Princess showed him the path without temper. Those who admired his courage then became his friends. It was they who helped him, not I or the Jade Emperor."

"She's Chinese. She doesn't belong there in Scotland."

"She belongs wherever her path takes her. And White Tiger didn't try to change her like you wished her to become your Monkey Queen. Instead, he wanted only to find out about her ways and her culture. That freed the Qi force."

Monkey King, feeling alone and sad, sat down, removed his crown and placed it in his lap. Scratching his furry head he stared at the crown. Why should he, the great Monkey King, have to suffer like this?

"Now you have two paths," continued Lord Buddha.

Monkey King looked up. He was fed up with all this talk about paths.

"You can throw away that crown and forget your palace and immortality, or you can put it back on, leap from my hand and start all over again. Neither I nor the Jade Emperor can make that choice for you."

Monkey King sat there for a long, long time, looking at his crown, wondering if there might be a third path ... to keep the crown but not on his head.

Lord Buddha read his thoughts:

"There is no third path, Monkey King."

Oliver Eade (www.olivereade.co.uk) writes for children, young adults and adults. *Moon Rabbit* (2009, second edition 2010) was his bestselling first published children's novel, followed in 2010 by *Northwards,* a dark fantasy set in North America (www.austinmacauley.com). *The Terminus,* a futuristic young adult novel set in London, is to be published in 2011 (www.littleacornpress.com) and *Elfink and the Baked Bean,* an illustrated story for younger children, in 2012. He is fond of fantasy and the mythology of different cultures.

Having lived in London, Southampton and America, he and his Chinese wife now stay in the Scottish Borders. They travel regularly to China where *Moon Rabbit* was conceived in 2006.

Alma Dowle, the illustrator, studied at Newcastle College of Art and loves illustrating children's books. Also a potter, she lives in the Scottish Borders where she taught art in primary schools for many years. Her joy is to draw and paint and share her gift with others. She was recently awarded a pass with distinction in children's book illustration from the London Art College.

For more information about the author, visit www.olivereade.co.uk

Visit White Tiger and Mei at www.moon-rabbit.org.uk